TRAVIS

BURNETT BRIDES CURRENT TIMES

SYLVIA MCDANIEL

VIRTUAL BOOKSELLER

Copyright

Copyright © 2022 Sylvia McDaniel
Published by Virtual Bookseller, LLC
All Rights Reserved
Cover Art by Dar Albert
Edited by Tina Winograd
ebook ISBN 978-1-950858-79-8
Paperback ISBN 978-1-950858-80-4

No part of this book may be reproduced, downloaded, transmitted, decompiled, reverse engineered, stored in or introduced to any information storage and retrieval system, in any form, whether electronic or mechanical without the author's written permission. Scanning, uploading or distribution of this book via the Internet or any other means without permission is prohibited.
Please purchase only authorized electronic versions, and do not participate in, or encourage pirated electronic versions.

❦ Created with Vellum

Secrets, Lies and a Matchmaking Ghost

Billionaire Travis Burnett would love to close the dude ranch portion of the Burnett Ranch. But the family board of directors refuses. So Travis must continue to deal with city slickers who think ranching is just riding horses and sipping cocktails in front of a fire.

He puts his foot down when ghost hunters want to explore the ranch. There are secrets that are better left hidden. Some secrets only the family knows. Some secrets even he wishes would go away.

As the star of her own ghost-hunting show, Samantha Rollins has always wanted to film the mysterious ethereal being she witnessed with her own eyes at the ranch. But one stubborn cowboy stands in her way. So now, after lying about her identity, she has a reservation at the dude ranch. She has her camera, her equipment, and she's covertly going to get the scoop on any paranormal activity.

What she didn't plan on was Travis Burnett awakening feelings she'd long ago given up on. She doesn't have time for love, especially with a man she's keeping secrets from. She has a ghost to catch and a show to promote. And no hunky cowboy is going to stop her.

CHAPTER 1

Travis Burnett glanced around the boardroom table at those gathered. It wasn't a fancy boardroom, but rather one filled with pictures of family members who had fought and struggled on the Burnett Ranch making it a success.

For over a century, they had worked cattle and made this outfit one of the most profitable and most lucrative in all of Texas.

Now twelve members all related to Eugenia and Thomas Burnett, who started the Burnett Ranch over one hundred years ago, sat around the table to make decisions about their commercial ranch. A dozen members who he often felt like throttling when they came before the board with their cockamamie ideas, who he knew many would disagree with his latest idea.

And still, he had to try. They had more than enough money. Why not focus on the cattle and horses? Especially now that they were talking about reality television shows coming to the dude ranch.

Not a good idea.

"Why in the world would we want to let a ghost hunting show come to the ranch?" he asked, wondering what they were thinking. Or smoking for that matter. "We don't need that kind of notoriety."

Most of the board members were in their twenties, all family with only two of the previous generation still making decisions about their corporation.

"It could draw even more attention and make us even more popular," his cousin Joshua said.

The fool must not have been visited by their great-great-great-great-grandmother. All they needed was for the television show to see her, and oh yes, they would most definitely be the most popular dude ranch in the U.S.—for all the wrong reasons.

"Have you been visited by the ghost?" Travis asked. Was he the only one of this generation who had seen her?

"You don't believe that nonsense do you?" Joshua said, his smile wide. "Come on, ghosts are not real. And if they are, we should make money on them."

"Yeah, they need to earn their keep," his cousin Cody said laughing. "We could make a lot of money on this show, and think of the free advertising."

"Think of all the looky-loos we'd get. Spend the night at the ranch and see a ghost," he said.

"She's not real," Justin said. "Eugenia Burnett Jones lives on because of her matchmaking reputation."

"How do you think your ancestors found love?" Aunt Rose asked.

"Oh, please," Jacob said. "If she was the matchmaker, why aren't you married?"

Oh, dear, that was not the way to get along with their aunt. The woman could be vindictive if she felt you were not supporting the family business the way she thought you should.

"We'll talk after this is over. I thought you would have known my story, but I'll be sure to enlighten you," she said, her face red.

That kid had a lot to learn if he wanted to stay on the board and be in Aunt Rose's good graces.

What could he say that wouldn't make him look like a fool? And yet they needed to know. Maybe if he admitted to seeing her, others would as well.

"I've seen her," he said, not wanting to admit to it, but knowing that some apparition had visited him and told him it was past time for him to remarry. "I'll give her your name the next time she comes to visit."

The damn ghost bothered him about once a week telling him about the latest guests that she thought would be a good match for him. And so far, he'd avoided all of them.

His cousin Joshua leaned back in his chair and laughed. "I didn't think you visited the bars. Did you hold a seance like our ancestor used to do?"

"I only drink at home," he said. "And no seances were held. Just wait, she'll come visit you. Then let's talk."

The man shook his head, but everyone else at the table

remained silent. They either had seen the ghost or they weren't saying. She'd been here for generations and even his father had confessed to seeing her.

"We don't need that kind of publicity," his aunt Rose said. "That could hurt our business."

The woman had never married, but rather made the ranch her permanent home and lived in the big house. Someday she would give it up, and Travis was next in line to live there.

But while the house had been remodeled, added onto, and made into a modern mansion, he would never move into the old homestead. A family needed to live in the house that had existed for over a hundred years. Since he never planned on marrying again, he would probably give it to his brother Tanner.

"Time to move on. I make a motion that we allow the ghost-hunting television show be allowed to film on the ranch," his cousin Jacob said, glancing at his brother Joshua with a grin.

"All in favor vote," Rose said. She was the head of the family and the corporation. Nothing got by this woman.

Only four of the twelve voted to allow them to film on the ranch. Travis smiled and decided it was time for him to make his desires known. It was time they realized what a pain in the ass the dude ranch had become.

He was tired of drunken guests, crying children, people ignoring the rules, and women who only came to go shopping in Dallas. People could be a real pain in the ass and so many that were sitting around this board didn't have to deal with them.

"Motion failed," Rose said, the oldest of the family there and the head of the directors. "The next item on the agenda is from Travis."

She gazed at him like he was the biggest pain in the ass of the group, but he knew that wasn't true. That was his cousin Cameron. That boy had tried the patience of all of them with his privileged behavior. Travis had taken his Corvette keys away twice and told him if it happened a third time, he'd take the car.

No one was allowed to drive drunk and Cameron did enjoy his beer.

All of their eyes were on him, wondering what he wanted this time. And they were going to be shocked.

"I'd like to make a motion that we close the dude ranch part of the business," he said.

They all stared at him like he was crazy. Several of his cousins leaned back in their chairs and laughed. Of course, they were the ones who did not work with the people. They were the ones who didn't have to put up with some of the stunts their guests had pulled.

"Why?" Rose, who was nearing seventy, asked. "We make good money from the dude ranch."

"Because I'm tired of dealing with the crazies who come here thinking they can be vacation cowboys. Someone is going to get seriously hurt and then we'll be sued."

"We have insurance to handle that," Aunt Rose said.

Justin shook his head. Travis's father, Mark Burnett, had taken the ranch into the modern day and upgraded their operations. But still, that didn't mean they needed the dude ranch. They were all extremely rich from the family business. Almost every Burnett had over a billion dollars in the bank thanks to their hard-working ancestors, great cattle, and even a little oil money.

His cousin Caleb shook his head. The boy had graduated college with a marketing degree and his focus was on getting them as much publicity as possible with a fancy website, newsletters, and Instagram and Facebook profiles. Not to mention the money he spent on advertising.

"I'm with Rose. Our profit margin is over fifty percent. People come here and enjoy riding horses, swimming, and our cookouts. We're in almost every travel magazine in the state of Texas and I'm attending a travel show next week in Washington D.C. that will showcase us even more."

Damn, this was not going well.

"Caleb, I'm glad you've made the dude ranch a big success, but I'm the one who has to deal with entertaining our guests and making certain that our clients don't do something stupid like try to tame a bull. That happened last year."

A smile crossed his cousin's face. "And you do a fine job of it. But we spent over twenty thousand dollars to get into these travel magazines. That would be a complete waste of money. I don't like to squander money."

Shit, this wasn't going well at all.

"Maybe, Travis, you should let the workers we hire do the trail rides and even the rodeo we host," Cody Burnett, Caleb's brother said.

Now that was just pure craziness. Neither one of them had ever worked the guest angle of the dude ranch.

"You would entrust our guests' safety to hired hands? Are you willing to risk us being sued?"

His brother Tucker who had been leaning back watching the interplay between the family finally spoke up. "I'm with Travis. Our guests need to be protected from themselves. That must always be something a family member handles. And a priority."

Oh, dear, his aunt Rose was frowning and she had that look on her face that implied you were suggesting they hire monsters. This was not someone you wanted to piss off and it appeared that Travis had just made her furious.

"The Burnett Ranch was established in 1870 right after the Civil War. My grandfather opened the dude ranch back in 1946 and saved our heritage with the money he made showing city slickers our life in the country. I'm never going to be for closing a piece of our heritage," his aunt Rose said, glaring at him like he was robbing the family silver.

The old woman had more money than any of them and no heirs.

"You're so right," his cousin Desiree said and Travis wanted to barf.

The woman worked in the front office and didn't know a thing about ranch life, though her father had been a great cowboy until an accident sidelined him. Now he sat on the board, but hardly ever said anything. He just let the younger generation make the decisions with Aunt Rose leading them.

"Any other discussion on closing the dude ranch?"

Everyone was silent.

"Let's vote," his aunt said.

There was no chance in hell this was going to pass, but he had to try for his own sanity.

"There are only three votes. The dude ranch will continue," his aunt said. "Next piece of business is the hiring of the new chef. She graduated from Escoffier in Boulder, Colorado, and is top rated."

Tanner raised his brows. "So why is she willing to come to a ranch on the outskirts of Texas? What have we got to offer? Why not some fancy-schmancy restaurant in New York?"

His aunt smiled. "Let's just say that she's had some bad things happen in her life and she needs a break from the hifalutin culinary world but wants to continue doing what she loves."

"Well, then she's not going to stay here long," Tanner said.

Travis remembered when she had flown down and toured their kitchen and cooked them a meal. The food had been excellent. Kind of frou-frou, but that's what people were expecting.

"Stop making assumptions, Tanner," Cousin Cameron said. "We don't know that. She may learn she loves Texas."

"No snow, warm winters, and hot-as-hell summers," Justin said.

Travis glanced at his brother and grinned. He'd just gotten his hand slapped by the next to youngest Burnett cousin Cameron and a smackdown from Justin. Desiree was the youngest, but that girl had a head on her shoulders.

"I make a motion that we hire her," Cousin Desiree said.

"Have we tasted her cooking?" Tucker asked.

"Yes, we had her out here a few weeks ago. You were in LA," Cody said.

That was the problem with Tucker. He had his own business to run and, oftentimes, he wasn't here when important decisions were made, though he did his best to attend every board meeting.

"Where was I?" Tanner asked.

Travis leaned over. "You were getting a checkup at the VA Hospital in Dallas," he said.

Tanner frowned and Travis knew he didn't like it when they talked about his PTSD. But the man had come so far from when he came home from the war.

"All in favor, raise your hands," his aunt said.

It was unanimous.

"She's hired. I'll have Katie send her the package offer. If all goes well, she'll be here in the next two weeks."

They all glanced around at each other knowing the board meeting was almost over and ready to get out of here. The small room was stuffy and he could hear the office staff right outside the doors keeping things running.

"I need someone to make a motion to adjourn the meeting."

His cousin Jacob spoke up and immediately they all voted on ending their once-a-month board meeting.

Once it was over, Travis slowly rose, knowing what he had to go do. It was past time and he wanted to get out there before they closed the gates.

"Gotta go," he told his family and grabbed his hat on the way out the door.

Shoving it on his head, he walked out to his truck parked not far from the office building.

Climbing in, he started up the vehicle and pulled out of the drive. As much as he hated cemeteries, he seemed to always find a sense of desolate peace when visiting.

It took him about twenty minutes to drive to the Riverdale Cemetery. When he pulled through the gate, the memory of the day of the funeral slapped him in the face.

Of standing between his brothers, staring in horror as they lowered her casket into the ground. The feeling of numbness that this couldn't be happening had overwhelmed him. In an instant, his life had changed forever.

Putting the truck in park and turning off the ignition, he reached for the flowers he'd bought and grabbed them off the seat.

As he climbed out of the truck, he glanced around at the barren place and the sense of sadness that seemed to permeate the air.

Walking up to the grave, he stared down at the tombstone. *Amanda Burnett and child. Taken Much Too Soon.*

With a sigh, he leaned down and took out the old flowers in the vase and put the new ones in. Every time he came here, his heart would ache with loneliness. Sorrow would fill his eyes with tears.

"God, how I still miss you. Our baby would be almost two years old. You two were my life and now I have nothing."

The wind blew and he heard the tinkling of wind chimes. It almost sounded like she answered him.

"I doubt you know I'm here, but still I have to come

check on you. Even if I'm just staring at a piece of rock with your name on it."

Slowly he rose. "Today, I tried to convince the family to close the dude ranch, but they weren't interested. I couldn't help but think about how much you loved the talent show. Without your touch, it just never is the same. God, how do I go on living without you?"

For almost three years, he'd asked himself that same question over and over.

He sighed and glanced around at all the tombstones. His heart ached with the sadness of this lonely land. Glancing over, he saw other family members, but he never thought to bring flowers to them.

Only Amanda and their baby.

Swallowing hard, he knew he had to leave. He couldn't stay long, it hurt too much.

"Gotta go, darling. See you next time."

Turning, he hurried to the truck, jumped in, and started the vehicle.

Damn, it just wasn't fair. They had loved each other since they were sixteen and their life together had ended way too early.

CHAPTER 2

Samantha Rollins sat in her beautiful office, going over where to shoot the next season of their show, Ghost Seekers. She knew exactly where she wanted the first episode of the new season to start, but where should they go after that?

Where else was there paranormal activity that had not been investigated thousands of times? In this business, you needed fresh, original destinations. Places that would produce proof that a ghost existed there.

The door to her office swung open and her pain-in-the-ass producer waltzed in unannounced. Not even a knock on the door. The man thought he was God.

His face was red, his eyes wide as he began to pace the length of her office.

"Samantha, you promised us this ranch, that we would get a celestial being on camera. For the last two seasons, you have gone to different places and we've captured nothing. Our viewers are tired and our rankings are slipping."

Being the pain in the ass he was, her stomach clenched. This wasn't news. In fact, he'd told her this multiple times to make her feel inadequate. What had set him off this time?

"Come in, Harry. I was going over the suggestions for our next few shows," she said, glancing up and glaring at him. "What are you talking about?"

"The ranch, they turned us down to get your ghost on tape."

What the hell? Why had the Burnetts turned her down? She knew a ghost lived there. She'd seen her. The memory was as fresh today as the echo of the children calling her ugly. Some hurts never went away and that one was painful.

"Shooting for the next season has to start in the next few weeks, and if it doesn't, then this show is over." Her director Harry Miller continued to pace her small office like a tiger trapped in a cage.

The only reason the Burnetts would turn her down was because they knew they had a ghost living on the ranch. This ghost was real and they didn't want it exposed. The billionaire ranchers had secrets. What else were they hiding?

The memory of the old woman shimmering before her as a young child returned filling her with warmth and determination. That one instance at their ranch was why she studied ghosts now. It was why she'd studied paranormal activity all her life that led her to become the host of Ghost Seekers.

The Burnetts were not going to undermine the career

she worked so hard to obtain. The career that ruined her marriage and left her like a princess in an ivory tower.

Maybe they wouldn't accept the show, but she could always return to the ranch without her crew. She knew how to operate the equipment. This was going to be her crowning achievement. Maybe even an Emmy was in her future.

"Relax, I think we can work around this," she told him, not certain if what she was considering was even legal.

But damn, chasing after ghosts enthralled her and she deserved happiness and the career she'd busted her ass to achieve. This career helped her to pack away the bad memories of her childhood and her ex-husband.

Nothing was going to stop her from getting what she wanted. Not even the rich and powerful Burnett family. And no question, their family was rolling in the dough.

All she wanted was a sampling of their success.

She glanced around at the office that had glass windows that peered down on 52nd Street in New York. It had taken her a lot of years to get here, and now as the host of her own ghost-hunting reality show, she wasn't going to be canceled or non-renewed even with a "boss hole" producer.

And Harry was the epitome of a bad boss. Barging in at any moment, checking up to make certain she'd done the work he requested. Changing things behind her back and telling the crew to do things she told them not to. If he learned there was something she didn't like, he made certain that's what the crew did.

So she had learned early on not to go directly to him, but to work around him to get what she needed.

There was no point in arguing with him. He was the producer, the director, and if he could be, the host as well. She'd learned this about him the first year they worked together.

"Relax? Did you just tell me to relax when this show is being considered for cancelation?"

It was best if she didn't react to him, but she would have a large glass of wine with dinner tonight. Somehow she had to soothe him and not let him see the fear rising inside her.

"I know the Burnett Ranch. I grew up close to where it's located. I'm going to call them and make a reservation for me, not the show, to stay at their dude ranch. I'll take my camera, my equipment, and I'll work undercover and get what I need."

Shaking his head, he stared at her. "Don't you think that will get us sued?"

"After I record her, I'll talk to them. Years ago, I knew the kids who lived there. Doubt they will recognize me. I looked a lot different then," she said, remembering how the kids at school used to bully her and call her carrot top, bucktooth, and a whole other assortment of ugly names.

Braces had changed the way she looked when she smiled. Her hair was now more of an auburn color and the ugly duckling she once was had grown into a beautiful swan that had her own television show. Fuck 'em.

"You said *her*," her produce said, his eyes narrowing. "How do you know the apparition is a *her*?"

This was the part that gave her confidence. "When I was nine, I met her."

"Come on," he said clearly not believing her.

Did this mean he was producing a show about ghosts and he didn't even believe in them? The man continued to surprise her.

"No, really. I ran into one of the cabins and she came to me and we talked."

No need to tell him that the reason she ran into that cabin was to escape the bullying of those mean kids. No need to tell him that she was crying her eyes out and that the ghost comforted her.

No need to tell him that the same bunch of mean girls still lived in the area. And she couldn't wait to show them that she had changed.

"You were nine. That's been years ago and this apparition may no longer be there," he said, shaking his head. "What about that hotel up in Colorado. Maybe we should go there."

That was not a bad place, but every ghost hunter in the country had been there. Few had captured anything on tape. At the Burnett Ranch, she really believed she had a better chance of meeting the grandmother's ghost again.

Enough of a chance, she was betting her career on it.

"Let me try this first, and if I fail, we can go to that hotel, but every ghost-hunting show goes there. That is not original. The Burnett Ranch has never been used. This will be new and fresh. Isn't that what we want to deliver to our audience, something they've never seen before?"

Funny how all it took were a few pertinent words and

already he was starting to come around to her way of thinking. *Fresh* and *new* were what every producer in the country was searching for.

A frown made his brows draw together as he stared at her. "How do I know you're just not trying to get a trip to your old hometown and hook up with an old flame?"

That had her laughing, especially at the memory of the kids bullying her. The only reason to return was the ghost. "There are no old flames. No exes. No one. Not even my family living there any longer. And I doubt that anyone will recognize me."

If it wasn't for the ghost she'd seen, she would never return to Texas and all the bad memories. It was there her father had passed away, leaving her mother and her destitute. It was there her mother had made the decision to return to the East Coast, closer to her family.

At the age of nine, it had been hard to leave one school and try to make friends somewhere else while still considered to be the ugliest kid in school. Bullies were not just found in Texas. Connecticut had its fair share of them as well.

But she'd shown them all. And now look at her; she had her own television show.

"You've got two weeks to get me footage that I can use on the show. If not, we're going to Colorado."

Even a deserted mining town in Colorado would be better than the hotel where a supposed murder occurred. But the hotel was a more popular destination and Samantha felt certain they would be shooting there as soon as she returned. Harry liked predictable.

"All right," she said. "I'll have my secretary make the booking as soon as possible."

"And I expect for you to check in with me daily and let me know how things are going," he told her. "Don't screw this up, Samantha."

Walking to the door, he sighed and turned to face her. "You're new in this business and while your beautiful face will entertain the audience for a while, sooner or later you must deliver."

He called her beautiful and warmth filled her. After being bullied so badly, she never got tired of someone telling her she was pretty. Even her boss hole producer.

"Yes, Harry, I'll get right on it," she said. "Don't worry, we'll get footage of the ghost."

What he didn't understand was her drive. After everything that had happened in her life, she had to be successful. No matter what happened, she would not let her show be canceled.

She would go to Texas, record the ghost, and then she would show her latest discovery to the world. After all, she'd met this ghost years ago, and because of her loving kindness, she'd become a ghost hunter. A ghost hunter with a television show.

An ugly duckling who became a swan just like the grandmother promised her.

CHAPTER 3

This morning, Travis was in the corral working the horses. As he put each horse through its paces, the sun rose high in the sky, reminding him that summer was only a week away.

Afterward, he planned on cleaning out the stalls and making certain the animals were all ready for the next round of guests coming in Saturday.

God, how he hated having to deal with people who had no clue about the dangers on the ranch, who treated his beloved horses and animals often harshly and mean which brought out the side of him the guests did not like. No one mistreated his horses, he didn't care who they were.

"Morning, Travis," Joshua, his cousin, said behind him. "Do you need any help today? Jacob and Justin are going into town to pick up supplies. Can they get you anything?"

Yes, he could use some help, but frankly, he didn't want to have to deal with their antics. Especially after the way they had acted at the board meeting.

It wasn't that they disagreed with him, it was the way they acted when he talked about their grandmother.

He stopped walking the horse in the coral and gazed at Joshua. "You know I don't drink and drive, so don't ever insinuate that I do ever again."

The boy's face turned red and he stubbed his toe in the dirt near the corral.

"Sorry, it just sort of slipped out," Joshua said. "I meant no disrespect."

"Well, that's not how it sounded."

After being a victim of alcohol, he seldom had a drink, and he would never get behind the wheel of a car with it in his system. A pain centered and began to throb in his chest. When would the pain go away?

"It's just I thought the ghost show would bring us more clients. We could make up something about seeing a ghost and tell them that a certain cabin was haunted. People love that shit."

Joshua was young. He had yet to see the ghost, but Travis felt certain that someday soon, their ancestor would show up on his doorstep. And Eugenia could only be seen by family members.

"What if they found something?" Travis said, the mare came up behind him and bumped him with her head wanting attention.

The kid didn't realize what the discovery of a real ghost would do to their business.

"No, there is nothing for them to find. No guests have complained. No one has said anything about seeing something or hearing things go bump in the night."

Maybe not, but Travis had spoken to her just last week.

The next time his grandmother Eugenia appeared before him, he was going to tell her to go visit Joshua. Let him see that they did indeed have a real ghost on the property. A relative who refused to leave even though she'd checked out.

How did he explain to a young person that their matchmaking great-great-great-great-grandmother was determined the family line would continue? And she would do everything she could to make certain her grandchildren married and had babies.

There was no convincing the young man. Not until he experienced her himself. And Travis couldn't wait to see his reaction then.

"Let's just agree to disagree. One day, you'll meet her and when you do, then remember this conversation."

The kid stood there for a moment and Travis could see he felt uneasy. And then he gazed at Travis with pity and he had to grit his teeth. Amanda and the boy had been friends, and though he didn't say it, Travis recognized the feelings of grief.

"Just don't want there to be any hard feelings between us," Joshua said, clearing his throat.

Tension seemed to radiate through Travis, and though he didn't want to be harsh, he couldn't help himself.

"Oh, there's not, because I'm right and you're wrong. You just don't realize it yet."

Joshua shook his head. "Damn, man, I miss Amanda too. Her death really changed you."

Like a slam to his chest, the words ripped at Travis's

insides and he had to fight to keep from succumbing to the grief. No matter how much time passed, he still had moments of numbing, paralyzing pain.

What did he expect when you lost the love of your life and your child? Good grief, this was why he didn't like to be around people too much. They got on his last ever-loving nerve. They reminded him of what he'd lost.

Turning back to his horse, he rubbed her nose, giving her the love she was seeking. Anything to gain control over his emotions. He didn't want to talk about Amanda to anyone.

"Run along to the accounting office, Joshua. I'm sure they're looking for you," he said gruffly, fighting to keep the tears at bay.

In a moment, he heard the man's boots crunching against the gravel and felt relief. He loved his family, but sometimes they could be the biggest pain in the ass.

Taking a deep breath, he got back to work again. This was where he found solace. Keep busy, don't think. Push on.

After each mare had her turn in the ring with him, he brushed them all down and gave them an extra helping of oats. Monday morning, they would be taking their guests on a trail ride and they deserved a little extra TLC for what they would have to endure.

Novice riders would kick the horses' ribs, pull their bits the wrong way, and generally be a nuisance. Because of their upcoming trials, he wanted to lavish them with love and attention today.

"Travis." Desiree entered the barn and called out

looking for him.

What now?

"Over here," he told her as he scooped a helping of oats into the feed trough for each horse.

"One of the maids called in sick. Can you help us get the cabins ready?"

"What about Caleb, Cody, or Cameron?" All the cousins who wanted to continue the dude ranch, but who never seemed to be available to take care of mundane chores.

"They're out riding the fence line, repairing the damage from the winter," she said. "I'm sorry. I wouldn't ask you, but you're the only one I can find."

Typical. How many cousins did he have and yet he was the only one who ran the damn dude ranch and kept it going?

"How many cabins?"

"Just two," she said. "My girls and I will do the rest."

"All right," he said. "This is why I brought before the board closing the dude ranch. No one seems to be around to help."

Desiree smiled at him sadly.

"That's never going to happen," Desiree said. "I understand your frustration, but Aunt Rose is never going to agree."

She was right. He'd probably been foolish for even trying, but he got tired of being the one who had to deal with the problems.

"You're right," he said with a sigh. "But I don't see her out here cleaning cabins and taking the guests on trail rides or teaching them how to rodeo."

Desiree walked over to him and touched him on the arm. "You do a really good job. And we all depend on you because we know the other cousins cannot be trusted to make certain it is done right."

It was true. They were younger and could not seem to stay focused on the job at hand. Once upon a time, he'd been just like them. But not anymore. Life had a way of making you see the bigger picture and what was important.

"Thanks," he said.

After she left the barn, he finished his work and then walked over to cabin five. Opening the door, he flicked on the light switch and began to clean the cabin.

While he was sweeping the floor, the smell of lavender filled the cabin and he sighed.

"Grandmother Eugenia, this is not a good time."

"Travis, dear," she said, shimmering before him. "Your wife has been gone for over two years. It's time you found another woman."

Good grief, that's all the woman wanted to talk about. Finding him someone. That would never happen.

"No, Ms. Eugenia, no more matchmaking. Amanda and my child were my life and now they're gone."

He glanced down to see she had placed her hand on his arm. While he couldn't feel anything, he knew she was there.

"Losing her was heartbreaking, but you are a Burnett. You must carry on the family name."

Laughing, he shook his head. "I have eleven cousins who all live here on the property to carry on the family name. One doesn't even believe in you. Why aren't you going to Joshua and telling him it's time to find a wife?"

The shimmer seemed to glow even more. "His turn will come. And he may not believe in me now, but that will soon change."

"Ms. Eugenia, Amanda was the love of my life and now she's gone. Go away and leave me be. Try your matchmaking on someone else. I'm never going to love again."

Suddenly his pail of water lifted and dumped over his head.

Curses filled the air as he blinked away the dirty sudsy water.

"Wake up, Travis. Amanda does not want you to never love again. Open your heart. This summer, I will find you someone, so you can quit being a stubborn Burnett and prepare to fall in love."

Wiping his face, he wanted to throttle the woman, but she was a ghost. He couldn't even catch her.

"Go away and leave me alone. Badger some other Burnett man. I'm never going to marry again."

How could the woman not see that all she was doing was upsetting him? All she did was remind him of how much he'd lost.

There was silence, and then suddenly, she rose above him. "I'm not giving up on you, and Amanda would not want you to be alone. I'll find someone for you to love."

With a swish, she left. The glowing aberration had disappeared and the smell of lavender was gone.

"I'm not someone you can fix," he yelled into the air. "I'm not a fixer-upper."

CHAPTER 4

Samantha gazed through the big windows of the guest check-in area at the Burnett Ranch. In the years she'd been gone, they had made renovations that made the place even more inviting than before.

Inside the room, big wooden beams held the roof up and there were western paintings and pictures of how the ranch had looked. It seemed almost every generation from the past was pictured on the wall.

Large windows were added to gaze out at the swimming pool, the barns, and even some cabins. The grounds were perfectly groomed and she could see workers hurrying back and forth between the buildings.

Big leather couches filled the lobby where guests could sit and wait for their cabin or their family to arrive. The opulence was daunting. The dude ranch was more like a resort than a ranch. Nothing like she remembered.

She had parked her rental car right outside the building, and now she was waiting to check in. Her secretary had been advised to ask for cabin five. That was where she had met the elderly woman who had comforted her. Though looking back, she sometimes wondered if she'd dreamed the entire event. At the time, she'd been so young.

The taunting by her classmates, she remembered very well. But what if the ghost she imagined was just a figment of her imagination? Then her career would be toast. She'd bet a lot on coming here and Harry the boss hole had made sure she knew before she left that he would be eager to walk her out if she didn't return with something incredible.

"Mrs. Rollins," a beautiful girl behind the counter called.

She stood and walked to her. "You're in cabin five. Here is your activity list. Tonight there will be a welcome reception here in this building and we'll be serving breakfast and dinner here as well. Lunch is served at the chuck wagon at whatever activity you're involved with. If you need anything at all, dial zero and we'll do our best to help you."

Her badge said Desiree Burnett and Samantha wondered how many family members it took to run this business.

"Thank you," Samantha said, eager to get to her cabin. It had been a long flight and then a two-hour drive just to reach the ranch, though they were but an hour from Fort Worth. The traffic from DFW airport was comparable to New York traffic in that it was often bumper to bumper. It had been years since she drove.

"Travis will take your luggage and escort you to your cabin. Enjoy your stay," the young lady said.

Like a flash from the past, she remembered Travis. He had been a year older than her and had been at the school outing saddling horses as they prepared to go riding that day. While everyone was occupied getting their mounts ready, the girls had gathered around her and taunted her until she ran from the barn to escape their mean, hateful words.

Today, those girls or women would never get away with their mean behavior.

"Good afternoon, ma'am," he said, picking up her suitcases. "Cabin five?"

"Yes," she said.

His face was still the same, though his eyes didn't seem to have the same fire they once held. Fear trickled down her spine and she wondered if he would recognize her. Doubtful. Her looks had changed that much.

Someday, she would return here and rub those hateful girls' noses in who she had become. But not this trip unless she had an opportunity.

"Please, call me Samantha," she told him. "*Ma'am* sounds like something you'd call my mother."

A smile spread across his face. "Just trying to be respectful."

"Be respectful by calling me Samantha," she said. "I'm not ancient yet."

"You look familiar. Where are you from?" he asked.

"The East Coast. Connecticut to be exact," she said, hoping he didn't remember her. Because then her job would be a lot harder. Especially if he traced her back to being the host of her ghost hunting show. Then her job would be impossible.

"Where are you from?" she asked, trying to be funny and stop him from thinking about what made her appear familiar.

A slow grin spread across his face. "Lived here my whole life. Seen some of the world, but always come back right here."

They walked toward the cabins and she liked the way he carried her heavy suitcases filled with equipment with ease. The man was muscular and strong as he walked across the gravel. Dark hair peeked from beneath his cowboy hat, and he had high cheekbones that held two small dimples. Long dark lashes covered his emerald eyes.

No longer did he look like a young boy, but rather a man who could handle whatever life threw at him.

"How long are you staying?"

"Just a week," she said, hoping she could get everything she needed by then. She had to be back in New York and preparing the episode or be looking for another job.

Besides, her boss hole producer would be setting up travel to other places and she knew she would find her show in Estes Park, Colorado. Beautiful, but been there, done that, and everyone's seen the results.

"The welcome reception will be in the building we just left at six o'clock this evening. People are normally tired and it doesn't last much later than eight, nine o'clock at the latest. It's just an opportunity to get to know all the guests who will be sharing this experience with you. Is there anything special that you're looking forward to doing?"

How about him?

God, she was exhausted. She would never think like that if she wasn't so tired. And it was the grandmother she was here to see, nothing else.

"Riding horses," she lied. "I'm not too tired for a chance to meet everyone."

Once again, she lied, and in fact, she didn't even want to attend the welcome reception, but felt like she had to, to keep up appearances.

He grinned at her. "The time difference will catch up with you. Don't drink too much alcohol because that will keep you awake."

Glancing at him, she wondered about him. Was he married? Did he have children? So much time had passed since she left.

"Are you going to be there?"

"All of the family is there the first night to welcome our guests," he said. "This week, even my brothers are both here."

She'd forgotten he had two brothers and cousins... Seemed like there was a whole passel of cousins. In some ways, she felt jealous. With no brothers or sisters, it had been her mother and a couple of cousins on the coast and that was her entire family.

And her cousins didn't have time for her.

Travis and she arrived at her cabin and she glanced around trying to remember what it looked like before. It had been so many years ago.

She went to put the key in the cabin, and as he tried to take the key from her, their hands touched. A zing of awareness traveled up her hand to her spine and then trailed all the way down to her center. Oh my. How long had it been since she felt those kinds of feelings?

Hell no. She didn't have time to be attracted to a rugged cowboy on the Burnett Ranch. Love had never been kind to her and she wasn't about to risk her career for a man. She'd done that once, gotten the T-shirt and then returned it. No more men. No more giving away her heart and definitely no more marriage. Stick a fork in her, she was cooked all the way through on men and love and marriage.

Travis Burnett was a hot hunk, but she was a cold dead fish inside.

"Let me," he said. "These old locks can be tricky."

He took her room key and slid it in the door. "We've been talking about upgrading to those new fancy ones where you just hold the card key against the lock, but we haven't done it yet."

The man smelled of leather and some other kind of smell that only Texas men seemed to have. She remembered her father smelling the same way and it caused a little catch in her throat. No, now was not the time to have memories of living here, not when she was gazing at a man's muscled back as he unlocked the door.

"They're nice," she said, trying to make small talk while she tamped down the desire she'd suddenly experienced. A cold shower would feel great about now.

While he held the door open, she walked into the room. It was a small combination of living room, bed, microwave and coffeemaker, and a big bathroom next to a small closet. Everything was different from when she ran in here at nine years of age. Of course, they had changed the room around and put in new furniture and linens. Even new curtains.

Nineteen years had passed. What did she expect?

He lifted her suitcase and put it on a luggage rack. She reached into her purse to tip him and he held up his hand.

"No, ma'am. We don't allow tipping on the property. Our guests have paid enough upfront and we don't expect a dime more."

The family was filthy rich; what was five dollars to them?

"Good, because you called me *ma'am* again. I'm only twenty-eight, not eighty. No tip for you."

A grin spread across his face. "Just being polite."

"Well, stop. It makes me feel old."

"You're not old," he said softly.

"No, I'm not."

"Do you need anything else?"

Oh, just for him to lay her down on the mattress, rip her clothes from her, and make love to her sex-starved body for the next eight hours. No lifetime commitment, just the two of them getting tangled in the sheets together.

But that wasn't possible and she pushed it out of her mind.

She glanced around the room, thinking about the last time she'd been here. "No. You've been a big help."

"Good. See you at the reception tonight," he said and walked to the door.

The back of his jeans hugged his ass like a fine pair of worn Levi's and she liked the way his shirt was starched and pressed with creases in the right place. His hat sat firmly on his head and his boots were of the finest quality leather.

And suddenly her breathing seemed to cease as he walked out the door. She hadn't reacted this way to a man in years. Now was not the time for her body to suddenly awaken from hibernation and decide that she needed sex. Just no.

Distance was what she needed to maintain from the Burnetts because she feared that once they learned what she was really doing here, they would not be happy with her.

If Travis learned what she was here for, she'd soon find herself out on the streets. If she didn't bring Harry back recordings of a ghost, she'd also find herself on the streets.

And what made her think doing this was a good idea?

As he closed the door, she moved about the room looking, searching for anything that reminded her of that day so long ago. Anything that would take her back and let her relive that experience once again.

Picking up a knickknack of a horse, she gazed at the piece of glass. Had it been here then? Shaking her head, she didn't know the answer. Nothing was the same. She wasn't the same. All she remembered was running in here and curling up in a ball on the floor between the bed and the wall, hiding, wanting to never return to the barn.

She opened her suitcase to begin to unpack and set up her equipment. No matter what, she needed to be prepared if the ghost appeared. Putting the camera on a stand, she hooked up the wires to her laptop and then set up the EMF meters. Next, she checked the filters on the video camera and white balanced for the dim lighting.

The smell of lavender filled the room.

What the hell was that? She hadn't gone into the bathroom. Did they have some kind of lavender potpourri?

A shimmer of light appeared before her and her heart skipped a beat. This was what happened last time. First the smell and then the light. Grandmother was returning and all Samantha could do was stare.

"Samantha, dear, how good to see you again," a voice said as the apparition materialized before her. "I've been waiting for you to return."

Stunned, Samantha stared at the ghost she'd seen as a child. It hadn't been a dream. This was real and she was speaking to her. Where was her camera? What the hell did she do now?

CHAPTER 5

Welcome parties were boring. At least, that's what Travis always thought. And tonight was no different. But it was a chance to get to know the people who were going to be spending the next seven days with him. The ones who laughed too much, drank too much, or stayed hidden in a corner.

Now was his time to put them on his checklists and make certain he was prepared when they suddenly grew stupid and thought that the bull in front of them wouldn't charge. Or that a rattlesnake bite was nothing worse than a dog bite. Or that the gentle horse they were riding would not take off across the prairie and kick them off her back.

If they were on vacation, they believed they were safe. Ha! That's when smart people did dumb things.

As he watched the guests mingling, his cousins dispersed among the people, talking and laughing, and he was so ready to go home. The reception building was the perfect place to hold this event with tables and chairs and even couches throughout the large room. The glass windows showed the moon sparkling on the pool, and outside, the lonesome wail of a cow could be heard.

This was the life he loved, but he could do without all the people.

"You're not smiling," Desiree said as she walked up to him. As his only female cousin, she looked gorgeous tonight in her long western skirt and boots. *Very chic* as Amanda would often say.

"What's to smile about?" he asked as he leaned against the wall. "This week, these people will drive me nuts."

"Even the red-haired woman?"

He turned and glanced at her annoyed. Every time they had a single female, his cousins tried to set him up. Maybe he was not handling their manipulation the right way. Maybe it was time for a more direct approach.

"Oh, she's going to drive me crazy. All that auburn hair flowing down her back. Her full breasts and tiny waist. And who could ignore those hips, full and shapely? I'd like to lay her down and—"

"All right, I get the point, smart-ass." A blush graced her beautiful face. His tactic had worked.

"Nothing has changed. I'm still never marrying again," Travis said with a smile. "Between all of you and the damn ghost, I should probably surrender and agree to marry someone, anyone, but that wouldn't be fair."

Desiree stood there for a moment staring out at their crowds. "Amanda would not want you to remain alone. She would want you to remarry."

"Well, she's not here to ask her about that, is she?"

Shaking her long dark hair, she stared at him like he had lost his mind.

"Damn, Travis, you can be the biggest pain in the ass," his cousin said, taking a sip of her wine before she walked away.

"Nice chatting with you," he said with a grin, knowing he'd gotten under her skin. Next time, she should not bring up Amanda or him finding someone else. In fact, maybe he should dictate a memo to all the family.

Leave me alone. I'm never marrying again. Stop with the matchmaking.

As Desiree walked away, she lifted her hand behind her back and flipped him off.

"Classy," he said loud enough just for her to hear.

Tonight he'd made a point of talking to every guest there. Now he needed to go back through and speak to each one again and then he was heading to his cabin. He'd had enough mingling with people for one night. Tomorrow the real challenge began.

Glancing at the crowd, he knew there were people here that would give him trouble. There were always one or two.

And yet, his eyes kept returning to Samantha. He liked her spunk and the way she had spoken to him. He liked the way the dress she wore flowed around her curves in a way that left him wanting more.

"Get your eyes off the redhead," Tanner said, walking up to him.

What was with his family tonight? Couldn't he look at a

woman without them thinking they were headed to the altar?

"Why? I can look, but I'll never touch," he said, watching her walk across the room and get another glass of wine.

He took a sip of his bottled water. Maybe she drank too much.

Tanner smiled at him, his dark eyes looked haunted. Travis knew that his brother was suffering, but he didn't know how to help him. The war had changed him into a man who seemed to always be brooding about something. He couldn't remember the last time he heard him laugh.

But then he also wondered if they thought the same thing about him. Did he brood like Tanner? His tolerance for idiots was a lot less than before.

"You should be out there flirting with the ladies," Travis said.

"Why? You think any of them want a broken soldier? Someone they can fix? I don't think so. It's safe being alone."

That was so true.

"Then keep your ass over here by me. We'll hold up the wall and be male wallflowers."

Tanner gave him a sly grin. "Now that's an idea I can get behind. It's about time for this party to start winding down."

"I'll say," Travis said, thinking this would never end. It was past eight o'clock. Time for these people to go to their cabins.

"What do you think of the new guests?" Tanner asked, taking a sip from a bottle of water.

Due to the medications he was on, his brother couldn't drink and Travis thought that was a good thing.

"This group of city slickers is going to test us," Travis said. "Already I can see some heavy drinking. And with that comes the fake courage to show how they could be a cowboy. That anyone can herd cattle and ride the range."

A sigh escaped from Tanner. "In the army, we called them short-timers. We knew those types thought they could kick ass and take names and soon they were carried out in a body bag."

Travis gave a little shiver. Seeing men die would have sent him over the edge. Having to identify Amanda's body left him with nightmares.

Tucker walked up beside them. "What are you pussies doing? Why aren't you out there entertaining our guests."

Just like him to walk up and chide them for not doing what he enjoyed. Tucker moved amongst high-powered men and women and thought nothing of it. While Travis just wanted to stay at home on the ranch and let the world pass him by.

"We're waiting on you," Travis said. "You're the hotshot who protects Hollywood, who enjoys parties. Tanner and I are the slackers."

"Yep," Tanner said as they all three stood and gazed out at their guests.

Tucker frowned.

"Funny. Does that redhead look familiar to you guys? Why do I think I know her from somewhere?"

Travis glanced at Samantha talking animatedly to a

man who could be old enough to be her father. "I thought so too, but she said she was from the coast. Connecticut."

Shaking his head, he studied her once more.

"Connecticut, Texas. There is a lot of road between the two. I think you're both just horny as hell and she's gorgeous," Tanner replied.

They turned and glanced at Tanner. "No."

Now, one of his brothers was trying to make something between him and Samantha. While he would admit she was beautiful, he met a lot of women that could be beauty queens, but that didn't mean he was interested in them.

"What? You gaze at so many beautiful actresses, that an ordinary woman is not good enough for you?" Tanner asked turning to Tucker.

"No. I'm busy and don't have time for a woman. But speaking of Hollywood. I just got a text. Seems my biggest client got herself into some real trouble and now her life is being threatened. I've got to get back to LA."

Travis shook his head and groaned. Why did it always seem to happen this way? "And here I thought you would take them all riding tomorrow."

"Not me," Tucker said. "Can you guys give me a ride out to the helipad? I need to get going if I'm going to make it back to LA tonight."

"Once again, I get stuck working the dude ranch," Travis said.

"Hey, I voted with you to close it down. We were the only three who wanted to close it," Tucker said.

"That's because we take care of the patrons and keep them safe," Tanner replied.

It was true. Tanner and Travis were the ones who made certain the guests went on safe explorations. They were the ones who kept the people in line, even when they were ready to kick them to the curb and leave them behind.

And tomorrow it all started over again.

The three men started toward the door.

"I was ready to ditch this party, anyway," Travis said, giving Samantha one last glance as he walked out the door. It was all right to look, just not touch. His brothers didn't notice him glancing back.

"Glad it's you getting on that helicopter. Had my fill of them in Iraq. Never want to fly on one again."

The three of them walked through the door and out into the night. The sky was filled with stars and a half-moon lit their way.

"It might be good for you to fly again," Tucker said to Tanner. "This time, there won't be bullets flying at you."

"No thanks," he said. "In my mind, I would start seeing and hearing the bullets hit the metal. I would relive the terror of thinking we were going down, certain we were all going to die."

"Shit," Tucker said. "That would scare me."

"Every time it happened, I would think I'm never getting on another helicopter. And then we would receive orders."

They all climbed up into Travis's truck and he started the engine and drove them to the helipad they had installed so Tucker could come and go with ease.

"I probably won't be back for a month," Tucker said.

"She's touring and I'll be traveling with her to make certain all the arrangements have been made."

Tucker had a job that Travis would never enjoy. The thought of being responsible for a celebrity and going from town to town sounded like a lot of work.

He pulled up to the helipad and saw the pilot waiting.

Tucker slid out of the truck and then glanced back at both of them.

"I'm going to see if I can find out who Samantha Rollins is. Something tells me she's from around here."

"All right," Travis said. "Keep in touch. We don't want to hear about you getting shot on the news."

His brother shook his head. "I will. Don't kill any guests while I'm gone."

"No guarantees," Travis said.

"I'll keep him in line," Tanner said to his brother.

"Gotta go, guys," Tucker said as he walked away and waved as he climbed on board.

They both sat in the truck and watched as the helicopter lifted and flew away.

"Son of bitch has the best job," Tanner said.

"Really? I was thinking it was the worst," Travis replied, glancing at his brother as he pulled the truck out onto the ranch road.

"Protecting beautiful women? I'd like to show them my weapon. It will keep them safe," he said with a laugh.

It was the first time that Tanner had expressed any emotions regarding their brother or women and Travis smiled. Maybe he was getting better.

The truck pulled up to the registration building. The

party was beginning to wind down and he could see guests leaving.

"Do we have to go back in there?" Tanner asked.

"No, I'm walking home," Travis said, thinking he would just leave the ranch truck at the recreation building.

Just then Samantha came out of the building. The lights shone on her enough that he could see through her dress. You could see her curves and he sighed at the sight. She glanced up at the sky, smiled, and then hurried to her cabin.

With a sigh, Travis watched her walk away. When she was gone, he turned back to see Tanner gazing at him.

"Brother, for the first time in years, you have that look in your eye. The one that says *there is a woman I desire.*"

Travis shrugged his shoulders. "My desire isn't dead. But I will never act on it again. Chasing a woman is over for me."

Tanner laughed. "I don't think so. Maybe you're finally coming back. Maybe there's hope after all."

"Don't count on it," Travis said, stepping out of the cab. He shut the door and began to walk back to his empty, lonely house. Back to safety where his heart could continue to grieve for the woman he loved.

CHAPTER 6

After the welcome reception, Samantha was anxious to get back to her cabin and hopefully speak to the ghost again. Quickly, she took a shower and prepped for bed, made certain her cameras were all recording, her EMF meter was turned on, and she even had a ghost box if needed.

Tonight she hoped to find out who the woman was and why she was still here and not resting in peace. There was so much she wanted to ask her and yet she hadn't appeared a second time tonight. Before she had not been ready to speak to her, but now that her equipment was recording, the ghost had yet to return.

Sinking down on the bed, she looked around the room and took a deep breath.

"Are you here? I'd love to talk to you some more. Get to know who you are. This afternoon, we barely said hello before I had to leave. Please come speak to me again."

She waited and nothing happened. Silence filled the air.

Sitting there, she felt like a fool. She was tired. It had been an extremely long day and she would like nothing better than to crawl beneath the covers and go to sleep.

With a sigh, she lay back on the bed and stared up at the ceiling. What did one do to make a ghost appear?

Her eyes grew heavy and the bed was so comfy. She dozed off to sleep and dreamed. Once again, she was that small child and the mean girls were teasing her about her ugly red hair. They were calling her carrot top and when they started making fun of her teeth, she turned and ran, tears rolling down her cheeks.

Why were they so mean to her?

The smell of lavender drifted to her nose and she jerked awake. Her EMF meter was flashing its lights and making an alarm that let her know a ghost was nearby.

Sitting up, she blinked and gazed about the room and turned the EMF meter down.

"Are you here?"

"Dear, you were having a nightmare," the ghost said, shimmering into view.

"Yes, I dreamed I was that little girl you rescued years ago," she said. "I was running to get away from the mean girls."

The woman sank down into a chair, her body shimmering. The clothes she wore were from back in the old days. At least the eighteen hundreds.

"What is your name?" Samantha asked. "And why are you still here? Why are you not resting?"

The woman laughed. "My name is Eugenia Burnett Jones. I lived a long time ago."

She was a Burnett. A family member. But why was she still here?

"Resting is boring. Besides, my family needs me. I thought my own sons were stubborn when it came to finding love, but this generation, they're impossible. What's happened to the world that young men and women think it's all right not to marry?"

She had no idea what year Eugenia had died. She didn't even know when she lived.

"When was your time?"

The woman wore a dress that came from a different time and place. "Honey, I buried my second husband in 1896 and I passed in 1899. We're buried in the small family cemetery here on the ranch. Lately, they've buried their dead in the town cemetery. But my bones are resting here on the ranch."

She had lived so long ago.

"That's over a hundred years," Samantha said stunned. "And you've been a ghost ever since?"

The apparition smiled. "Oh no, I rested for a while, but every so often I liked to check on my grandkids. My great-grandkids, great-great-grandkids, and now I'm dealing with great-great-great-grandkids. They're a handful."

Samantha was so happy that the camera was recording her. She was getting all this information on tape. It would be a great show.

"Men just don't change. Soon, I saw the same pattern that my sons pulled. If this family is going to survive, I had to come back from the dead to help these boys find their mates. And that's what I'm doing."

Oh, my God, Eugenia was playing matchmaker with her descendants. Matchmaker to her grandkids. It was all Samantha could do not to laugh. Who would have thought that a ghost would return to make certain her family was continuing the family line?

"What's all this stuff you have set up in this room?"

What did she do now? If she told her the truth, she feared that the ghost was going to disappear and she'd never see her again.

"It's monitoring equipment," she said. "It keeps track of things."

The woman frowned. "What happened to you after you left the ranch that day? I haven't seen you in almost twenty years."

After the school outing at the ranch, summer arrived, and then her father had been killed. That summer was the year she felt like she grew up. That year, not only did she have to deal with mean girls, but life-changing events that shaped her forever.

"My father was killed in a bull riding accident. He had been a professional rider up until the day he rode his last bull. Not long after he died, my mother sold everything, and we moved to Connecticut to be near her family. She still lives there," Samantha said.

There was so much more to this tale, but she didn't tell her about how changing schools had only made her realize that bullies lived everywhere. That when one parent died, everything changed including their finances. Times had grown hard and her mother had trouble for many years.

"I'm sorry to hear about your father," Eugenia said.

"Yes, I think our life would have been different if he had lived," she said, remembering the times they barely survived on her mother's salary. How grief nearly destroyed her mother.

It was during this time she'd made the decision she would go into television and be a ghost hunter on the side. Braces had straightened her teeth and somewhere along the way, her hair had become darker. Her complexion cleared and her facial features matured. The chubby little girl slimed down and the woman emerged.

The ugly duckling had turned into a swan who hated mean girls and would no longer accept their bullying. In college, she'd become the girl most sought after and would never be friends with anyone who picked on someone less fortunate.

"So how are you matchmaking your family? Isn't it hard since you're a ghost?" Samantha asked suddenly interested in who she was trying to match up. "Who is your target?"

The thought of getting evidence of a matchmaking ghost had Samantha suddenly all excited. It would make great reality TV.

"None of this generation has married, yet. Well, Travis was for a while. I've been talking to Travis and Tanner and I keep trying to catch Tucker, but he's not here at the ranch that often. But sooner or later, I'm going to have a little chat with him. Then there are the others. Right now I have twelve men and women that I'm working on finding them someone to love."

"But how? You're a ghost. It's not like you can introduce them to women," she said.

Already she could see herself accepting an Emmy award for best reality show. This matchmaking grandma was going to take her career to the next level.

"That's the hardest part. I'm restricted to this area, so it has to be someone who comes to the ranch. Someone who I think is a good quality person who will have their best interests at heart. And believe me, I know how to get their attention. I have my ways."

Eugenia glanced about the room. "The guests are usually not too pleased when I appear. So I have to try to get them together without appearing. Or if I do show myself to them, then the family gets mad when the guest goes running out of the cabin screaming."

Samantha giggled. "That could be bad for their business."

"Pfft! Business, that's all they think about. Besides, this generation has more money than they know what to do with. I can't even imagine the money they have. They need to spend more time with their family. They need to be busy creating families."

Family was something that Samantha really didn't have much of. Her mother had a sister, her grandparents were dead and she had a couple of female cousins who spoke to her when they gathered, but they were not close. With no brothers or sisters, she wouldn't know the meaning of having a close family.

"They don't realize how lucky they are to have each other," she said softly.

"Exactly, and that's why I'm here. To make certain the family line never ends. That each one of them finds someone to create a family with. Babies. We need more babies. My sons knew I wanted grandbabies and this generation seems uninterested in having children. So I'm here to make certain there is another generation behind this one."

Oh dear. The thought of a mother telling her children she wanted grandbabies was hilarious. Thank God her own mother warned her against having children.

"So who have you picked out for each one?"

She grinned. "I'm still working on it, but I think I know about Travis. Tucker is still a work in progress. And Tanner…" she shook her head. "That boy is just like my son that was named Tanner. The war did horrible things to his mind and it took a long time to bring him back. But when the right girl comes along, she'll help heal him."

It sounded like Tanner suffered from PTSD and that was not something a wife could heal. Only time and distance from the war seemed to be what helped those men.

Samantha remembered seeing Tanner at the welcome reception and even the other man Tucker. But weren't there more family members? She remembered meeting several other Burnetts.

"What about the others?"

"Oh, in time I'll find just the right person for them. Right now, I'm concentrating on the three boys who remind me of my sons. They're the oldest and it's past time for them to have a wife and even children."

Suddenly there was a knock on the door.

They glanced at one another and Eugenia dissipated.

With a glance out the window, Samantha realized it was past dawn. It was past time for her to be down at the barn.

"Shit," she said out loud.

"Watch your language, sweetie," Eugenia said.

Looking around, Samantha knew she was no longer visible and she certainly didn't want anyone to come into her cabin and see her equipment.

When she reached the door, she pulled it open just wide enough to see who was there.

Travis stood there leaning against the post, his hat pushed back and a smile on his face.

"Did you oversleep? It's time for our trail ride."

"Oh, I'm sorry, why don't you go on without me," she said, thinking she wasn't finished talking to Eugenia. There was so much more they needed to cover.

"Nope, this is the first activity of the day, the horse is saddled and waiting on you. Time to go," he said. "We'll give you five minutes to get dressed."

With a grimace, she knew she had to go.

"All right," she said. "Let me change clothes."

"Cute pajamas, by the way," he said and turned and walked off.

Stepping back inside she glanced around. Eugenia was gone.

"Eugenia?"

Nothing. The woman had disappeared and now it was time for Samantha to go horseback riding.

"What time is it," she said out loud.

Glancing at the clock, she realized they had spoken for hours.

Running around, she grabbed her clothes and brushed her teeth before she walked out.

She couldn't wait to get back and check the footage to see what it showed. Maybe she would send her boss a little sliver of recording to show him what she had so far.

Maybe, she thought as she walked out of the cabin. Grabbing her phone, she sent him a quick text.

Footage…coming soon.

CHAPTER 7

*T*ravis grinned as he walked back from Samantha's cabin, his boots crunching on the gravel. Those sexy little pajamas she wore had teased him with just a hint of her nipple shining through, the thin straps sliding down her shoulder, and the way the silk clung to her body.

Even now, he had to talk his manhood back down. The red-haired beauty was stunning. Standing there, he'd gazed at her long legs and sheer silk pajamas like a starving man. But just because the buffet was open didn't mean he had to partake.

When he got back to the corral, the other guests were being helped onto their horses. Cody and Cameron were matching each guest to a horse. As much as he loved his cousins, he always went behind them to make certain they had picked the appropriate horse for the client.

"Miss Samantha will join us in a few moments," he said.

"Excuse me," Mr. Stephens, the one he'd labeled a troublemaker, stepped in front of him. "I'd like to ride that horse you have in the coral outside."

Jockey, their male stud was not safe to ride.

"I'm sorry, but we don't allow guests to ride him. He's only ridden by the family and to be honest, we all avoid him."

The man's brows drew together and he frowned. "I've been riding horses all my life and I'm quite capable."

"I'm sure you are, but Jockey is not to be ridden."

It was best if he walked away because he could see the man preparing his next arguments.

"Enjoy your ride," he said as he walked to the chuck wagon and saw that Tanner and Desiree were busy loading up the coffee and all the breakfast goodies.

Glancing around at the guests, he recognized the ones who had been around horses before, the greenhorns, and the most dangerous – the one who demanded obedience over beast, Mr. Stephens.

Those he disliked the most.

"I'm going to put you in the order I want you to ride in. Desiree and Tanner will be in the back and that's where I want my beginners. They will help you and even ride alongside you. Next, I want my intermediate riders."

The one among the guests that he knew would cause trouble frowned.

"We can't just ride on our own?"

"You are riding on your own, but we're on a trail ride and I want us to stay in line as much as possible," he said. "We could encounter snakes or skunks or coyotes. I'd like to have us all together to keep us safe. Your safety is important to me and my staff."

Good grief, already he could tell this man would be big problems.

Samantha walked up and Tanner spoke to her and then helped her up on a horse. She held the reins like she knew what she was doing and even sat in the saddle in a manner that gave him hope.

Walking over, he pulled her in behind him. "Good morning, sunshine."

"Sorry, I overslept," she said. "That flight from New York was a long one yesterday."

That was probably true. "Stick in close behind me. You have ridden before?"

"Oh, yes," she said, and from watching her, he knew it was true.

He glanced behind him and saw that everyone was sitting on their horses waiting on him.

"All right, let's go," he said and climbed into his saddle on his trusted roan and began to lead the way. "First stop, the cemetery."

He led the procession of horses down the road. The staff knew to stay off this road today. They were given a list of the activities and were told to do their best not to get in the way of the guests.

"What a way to start the day," the grumpy man said. "A cemetery."

"The cemetery holds our ancestors. From the first people who started the ranch to my mother and father," he said, hoping the man would shut up or he'd be tempted to punch him. "We're not going to get off our horses. Just stop and let you see the headstones. Honor the pioneers who started the Burnett Ranch."

He had chosen not to bury his wife and child here, but rather put them in her family plot out in the city cemetery. Sometimes he regretted his decision, but he knew she would want to be beside her parents, and though he never intended to remarry, you just never knew.

"Over here is Thomas Burnett and his wife Eugenia. Many years after his death, she remarried. He is buried on the other side of her. The way they met was that she kept sending widow women with casseroles to his home. After his death, her sons bought his ranch and it became incorporated into the Burnett Ranch."

They rode farther down the road and Travis glanced back to make certain the first-timers were doing all right. Tanner and Desiree were working with them and the horses they had chosen for them were some of the best-trained on the ranch.

Along the road, he pulled his horse to a stop and then spoke loud enough so everyone could hear him.

"As you can see, the ranch hands are out in the fields working the crops. We grow cotton, wheat, and maize. If a field is empty, it's because we're letting it rest. We also have over a thousand head of cattle that we move around. The life of a rancher is to work from sunup to sundown and is not a life of luxury, by any means. We are fortunate that our ranch is profitable, but that's because of the work of our ancestors," he said, thankful they had made the ranch into the well-established enterprise it was today.

One of the horses let go a big fart and the women behind it started laughing. When it stopped and started peeing, he turned around to see Desiree give the animal a little push to get the rider going again.

"He needs to learn some manners," the woman said.

"Honey, I don't think animals care," her husband told her.

They rode along and he pointed out the different trees that grew on the ranch. "Next up, we're going to stop at the top of the mountain cliff and have breakfast. We are in rattlesnake country, so be on the lookout among the rocks. Let me get off my horse and look around before any of you get off."

Glancing at Samantha, he noticed that she swayed in her saddle and her eyes were droopy like she hadn't slept much last night.

"You going to make it, sleeping beauty?"

"Yes," she said with a sigh. "But a nap is in my future. A cup of coffee would be heavenly right now."

"Coming up," he said, pulling his horse to a stop at the top of the small incline. For the most part, the ranch was flat, but there was this small hilly section that looked down on the rest of the ranch and he liked to stop here for breakfast.

The grumpy man was swinging his leg off his horse.

"Sir, wait just a minute and let me check the area out," Travis warned him. "You don't have boots on and I do. One strike and you could be dead."

The man's face turned white, and he shook his head like

it was an imposition, and yet he would be the first one to sue them if he was bitten by a rattlesnake.

Travis stepped down and walked around the area, especially near the rocks that leaned out over the ridge. Then he helped pull the chuck wagon into position.

"All right, folks, step out of your saddle."

Years ago, they had put up a portable latrine here and he quickly checked it for snakes and then some of the ladies went into the smelly outhouse.

The first-timers were walking around trying to get the aches and pains out of their legs. Stradling a horse could make a person sore if you hadn't ridden in a while.

"Breakfast should be ready in a few moments," he said and went to help Desiree and Tanner get everything prepared.

"Excuse me," the grumpy man said, pulling him aside. "Why can't we go riding on our own? I'd like to take off across those fields and see what's on the other side."

There was always one who wanted to break the rules.

"Mr. Stephens, if you ride your horse across our cotton you're going to be destroying crops. If you want to go riding, let me know and I can arrange for someone to go with you, but we never let our guests out riding by themselves."

The man snarled. "Then what's the point of coming to a dude ranch if you can't go horseback riding and race across the fields."

Travis took a deep breath.

"Your safety is the most important thing for us. You're

welcome to go for a ride as long as one of us is with you," he said.

Turning, Travis walked away knowing he needed to get far from the man.

Samantha approached him and handed him a cup of coffee. "I thought you could use this."

He grinned at her remembering the way she had looked this morning in her pajamas.

"Thank you," he said. "You're the one who slept too late. I should be bringing you coffee."

"No, you earned it. That guy is a dick," she said. "It's black. No cream or sugar," she told him sipping from her own cup.

Her tongue ran across her full cherry lips, and for a second, he wondered how she would taste. But he would never know because he would never kiss her.

As much as he wanted to respond and agree with her, he was silent and spoke only about the coffee. "That's just the way I like it."

They walked farther away and he sighed.

"Deep breaths. That's what I say when my boss hole walks out of my office."

"Boss hole?" he asked, surprised at the name.

"Yes, that's my pet name for him. I thought it was better than something else I could call him, though that was more of what I wanted to say."

A chuckle bubbled up from his chest, leaving it warm.

"What do you do?"

"I'm in television," she said. "It's all about the ratings. And he would do anything for higher ratings. Including selling his soul to the devil if it made him the number one show."

A strange feeling overcame him. There was something about her that seemed like it was just on the edge of his mind. Like he knew her and yet he didn't know anyone in television.

"Would I recognize you on television if I saw you?"

"Probably not. I am in front of the camera sometimes, but mainly I work behind the scenes. It's only when I'm doing special reporting that people see me."

Why did he feel like he was not getting the whole story? It was like she didn't want to tell him what show she worked on.

Suddenly a woman came running out of the porta-potty screaming. He shoved his cup of coffee at Samantha and took off running. Desiree beat him there.

"What's wrong?"

"There's a big spider in there," she said, visibly shaking.

Good grief. And they wondered why he wanted to close the dude ranch.

He opened the door and a daddy longlegs crawled down the door. With a swipe of his hand, he sent the spider flying into the woods.

"He's gone."

Desiree gave him a look that clearly said *have patience*, but his was running thin. Between the grumpy man who wanted to race across their fields and the women who couldn't handle a spider, he was ready to call it a day.

"Breakfast is served," Tanner called.

Travis found Samantha holding his coffee, laughing.

"You just saved mankind," she said.

With a sigh, he shook his head. "Samantha, it's time for you to get some breakfast."

"Yes, sir," she said. "Are you serving up spiders?"

"Good God, no," he said. "The health department would never approve."

The gaze she sent him had his insides heating up. "Too bad."

As she walked away, he took deep cleansing breaths. All he could think about was how she looked in her pajamas this morning.

CHAPTER 8

The next morning Samantha and Eugenia were talking in the cabin when her cell phone rang.

"What's that?" Eugenia cried, floating up into the air obviously spooked.

"Trouble," she said, glancing down at her phone. She shook her head and watched as the ghost disappeared.

Did he not understand that he was costing her precious time with Eugenia? She answered the ringing phone.

"Harry, I'm busy. You just interrupted a session with the ghost. I'll call you; don't call me," she said into her cell phone, irritated. She and Eugenia had been conversing about the value of family.

Harry's timing was terrible. In fact, most men's timing really sucked. Especially her ex-husband. The memory of walking in and finding him with his mistress slammed into her. Not that she cared any longer, but rather just the way he had informed her of their pending divorce.

Once again, she and Eugenia had been interrupted.

And, sadly, Eugenia had been telling her about her second husband Wyatt and how she used to send women to him with casserole dishes. Until the day he confronted her and told her the only woman he was interested in was her.

Listening to her tale had been so interesting. Yesterday, she'd seen the graves of both of them.

"Samantha, if you were sitting on my side of the phone, you would understand why I think you need to see a shrink when you return. Do you know how that sounds? I'm not believing you."

"You're the producer of a ghost hunting show," she said.

"I don't have to believe in ghosts," he said. "You, though, need to produce proof of one and soon."

The man was indeed a boss hole and she was biting her lip to keep from calling him one now.

"That's what I was working on when you called and interrupted us. That's what I was sent here to do, and now you're telling me I need to see a shrink. Well, make the appointment, but it won't be the ghost we'll be talking about, it will be you."

The man chuckled. "Down, girl. You know I only have your best interest at heart."

His tone had changed from confrontational to sweet like he was trying to make her understand he was only looking out for her. What a lie.

The words almost slipped from between her lips, but thankfully, she stopped them just in time. But she could still think it and she called bullshit. His only concern was giving the network what they wanted.

"Of course, you do," she said in that sweet-tea-and-bullshit way women could talk that let you know exactly what they were saying. If he could talk crap so could she. "Bless your heart, and you probably are interviewing people to take my place even now."

Over the phone, she heard coffee spewing. Yep, exactly what she thought. He would sell her out before the ink dried on her next contract.

"Just remember the clause I put in my contract that my salary will double if you betray me and I learn you've hired someone else before I leave the show. And I would really like to be making double what I am. Maybe then I could afford a nice beach house in the Hamptons."

There was silence on the other end of the line. "There is no such clause in your contract because the network would never allow it."

She laughed. "I have a damn good agent. Gotta run, Harry, it's my turn to collect the eggs and the ladies are waiting for me."

"Call me later today," he said.

"If I have time," she replied. "I've got a ghost to record. If I'm not interrupted. Celestial beings don't like it when modern technology intrudes."

She disconnected the line and glanced down at the phone. "Boss hole."

Quickly she dressed, knowing she would be collecting the eggs this morning. She wasn't afraid and Desiree would be there with her. She had collected eggs many a time when she was a child before they moved off the ranch her father owned.

With a sigh, she knew she wanted to go back and see

the old place and even visit her father's grave, but she would need to time it perfectly so that no one learned who she was.

Walking out the door, she headed toward the hen house and sighed. Being here, she was quickly learning there were things about Texas she had forgotten. Things she missed: the clear blue skies in the morning and the heat of the sun, though she knew come August, it wouldn't be heat, it would be hell creeping up from below.

Travis leaned against the hen house and she frowned. The man looked damn good with his perfectly pressed jeans and boots and his shirt outlining the rigid muscles of his chest. This was man candy and she wanted a big ole bite.

"Good morning," she said. "Where's Desiree?"

He stood and stretched. "Good morning, sunshine. She had some things she had to take care of this morning and asked me if I could help you collect the eggs."

Glancing around, she wondered where the others were.

"Am I the only guest who is doing this wonderful chore?"

"No, tomorrow morning, Mr. Stephens is going to get the chance to stick his hand in and find the golden egg. Today is all about you."

She smiled. "Well, won't that be fun? Be careful, he'll steal the goose that laid the golden egg."

A grin spread over his face. "There's always one who keeps things interesting."

The memory of bringing in the eggs and washing them made her smile.

"I just bet you hope that egg has chicken shit on it," she said, gazing at him with a serious expression on his face.

He busted out laughing. "Never. He's a guest and we never wish bad things on our patrons."

"Yeah, right," she said. "Don't lie to me. I call bullshit."

A grin spread across his face. "Come on, let's get this over with, so we can have breakfast at the reception hall. I'm a little hungry this morning. Then you can go do arts and crafts."

"Joy of joys," she said.

Picking up a basket, she gazed at the supplies inside the little house. "No gloves?"

"Nope," he said. "The girls don't need to peck at the rubber gloves and choke on plastic. It's not part of their food."

Chickens stunk. And this morning, only about four were still sitting on their nests. The rest were out in the pen, squawking and digging in the dirt. Why were these four lovelies just waiting to taste her blood?

"Let's do this," she said and took a step toward the first nest. The roosts were arranged in rows and she walked down the first one.

"You act like you've done this before," he said, watching her.

"There are chickens and eggs back in Connecticut."

Peering into the nests, she found about a dozen eggs and came around to the chickens who were still sitting on the roost.

"I bet Connecticut eggs aren't as good as Texas ones," he taunted.

"They taste the same. Only in some parts of the state, they're a little richer," she said.

Turning to the next row, she faced the hens still on the nests.

"Hello, ladies, thanks for donating your eggs. I'm here to collect. So give them up," she said and reached beneath a hen, who reached out and pecked her.

"Not nice," she said. "But I got it anyway. Sore loser."

"Myrtle is always a bit nasty," Travis said. "She's a bit cranky."

"Well, thanks for the warning," she said. "Someone should put her in a pot. That would teach her."

She went to move to the next hen and a rattle startled her. That deadly sound sent a shiver down her spine. Glancing down she saw her worst nightmare – a rattlesnake all coiled and giving her a warning before it struck.

Travis grabbed her arm. "Don't move."

Her heart was pounding in her chest as she and the snake stared at each other. Its cold eyes and darting tongue had fear roaring through her like a freight train and she was ready to jump the tracks. But knew it would strike if she moved.

"I'm not ready to die," she said with a nervous whisper.

"Good. I'm not either," he said, slowly reaching behind him.

"What's on your bucket list?" he asked.

What was wrong with this man? They were facing death and he wanted to talk about the things she wanted to do before she passed?

"You want to talk about my bucket list when I'm staring at death?"

"Sure," he said. "I want to go to Alaska. That's one place I haven't been yet."

She licked her suddenly dry lips, thinking the man was nuts for talking about visiting a state. What was on her bucket list now that she was close to dying?

"Work on a show that reaches number one in the ratings and tell my boss hole I'm the reason he's doing so well," she said, fearing that at any second, she would feel that snake's teeth sink into her leg.

"Why? Tell me why that's on your bucket list? Why not a trip or a husband or children?"

"Because I suck at marriage," she said, wondering why at this moment she would tell him something so personal.

He laughed. "You suck at it, and I did really well, only fate had something different in store for me."

What did he mean by that? She knew he was no longer married.

"Oh, did your wife get bitten by a snake?"

"No," he said, but he didn't tell her what happened and she wondered, though right now her focus was on not moving.

"Why do you suck at marriage?"

Oh, that was easy and gut wrenching at the same time.

"Because my career came first. He came second and his mistress came third. End of story. End of marriage. They are happily fornicating forever after."

There was silence in the hen house, except for the

continued rattling noise. If one of these hens moved, that snake would attack and she'd be a dead woman.

"Don't move, I'm almost there," he said. "When I say run, you get out of here."

"What about you?"

"I'll be fine," he said. Fear for them both seemed to explode inside her and she didn't want him to get hurt.

Suddenly he brought down a shovel on the snake's head, trapping him. "Run."

She didn't think twice and hauled ass out of the chicken shed as fast as she could. She hadn't moved this fast since she was sixteen. Once outside, she started screaming as she ran toward the barn. Not knowing where exactly to go.

Who could help Travis?

Tanner who had been in the barn came to the door.

"What's wrong," he asked.

Suddenly she tripped and the basket of eggs went flying. The morning's work lay in a scrambled heap in the dirt. All that work and one rattlesnake had ended it all.

"Rattlesnake," she cried. "Travis is killing it."

Tanner walked over and helped her up.

"Are you all right?"

"I'm fine, go help Travis," she said breathing hard, dusting her jeans off.

He glanced down at the scrambled eggs that now lay in the dirt.

"Damn, that was supposed to be breakfast," he said with a chuckle.

"Screw breakfast. I'll order us all takeout. I don't care.

But your brother had that rattler trapped beneath a shovel. Go help him."

Just then Travis walked out of the hen house with the dead headless snake in the shovel.

"Whoa," Tanner said. "That's a big one. We can have rattlesnake barbecue tonight."

"That's a great idea," Travis said.

Staring at the two men who were grinning like they had just captured a delightful meal, she began to shake from the inside.

"You people are crazy," she said, staring at the three-foot-long snake that could have ended her life.

The tremors began on the outside. She'd never been so frightened in her life.

This day had started out like crap with the phone call from Harry, the rattlesnake, and she'd broken all the eggs.

"Hey, are you okay," Travis asked her and handed the shovel to Tanner. "Take that to the cook."

Tears welled up in her eyes and her knees were knocking together so hard, she feared she'd fall down. "No. I don't like snakes. They're evil. I've never been so scared in all my life."

In two steps, he was by her side and pulled her into his arms. "It's okay. We're both fine. Neither one of us got bitten and if I had been paying more attention to the chickens than you, I would have realized something was wrong. That's why they were still on the roost."

Had he been paying attention to her instead of the chickens?

"But the eggs," she said with a whimper against his chest.

The feel of his big strong arms around her was comforting. Soothing in ways she'd long forgotten about. And he smelled like a strong, manly man who she could depend on.

"Forget about the eggs. It doesn't matter. Just think now you can return to New York and say you came eye to eye with a rattlesnake."

Hell, she worked with a rattlesnake. But this one terrified her. One more step and it would have struck. One more step and she'd been on a stretcher in an ambulance on her way to the hospital.

"Why didn't this happen with Mr. Stephens," she said. "Not that I want to wish this off on anyone."

Travis started to laugh. "He'd be dead. Because he would not have listened. He would have run out of there and that snake would have struck him and probably me as well. You're brave and you did what you needed to do to survive."

It was then she realized she was still being held in his arms. She could feel his chest against her breast and the way he smelled of leather and some smell that seemed to light her internal fires. Something she had no business experiencing. Ever again.

That all her lady bits were singing the songs of her ancestors at being reawakened. Was this part of being on a ranch? Reconnecting to the past in ways she'd never dreamed of?

Oh no, this couldn't be happening.

Stepping back, she glanced at him. "Thank you. But I think I need to change my clothes. Not only did I fall, but I was so scared, I think I peed a little."

Travis leaned his head back and laughed.

"Excuse me," she said and hurried away.

No, she had done nothing of the sort, but she needed to get away from him as quickly as possible. Because he had aroused in her all the emotions that she ran from. This was not the time or the place to suddenly have her body awaken to the feel of a man holding her.

Especially not a big, handsome man like Travis who seemed to have awakened the long-hidden woman in her. That person she thought had been buried, never to return when she signed the divorce papers.

CHAPTER 9

*L*ater that evening, Travis sat watching mindless television, trying not to think about how close Samantha had come to getting bitten by a rattlesnake. Snakes loved chicken eggs and he didn't approve of letting their guests go in, but the board had told him he was being too cautious.

Well, wait until they learned of this little incident. Snake anti-venom was in short supply and what if Samantha had died from not being treated. All the scenarios went around and around in his mind, and he had to stop himself and remember he had killed the snake.

Samantha was safe. And he'd even got to hug her while she shook. The feel of her in his arms had sent his mind into overload. She fit right there and it had been so good to hold her and smell her and realize that a woman belonged in his arms.

With a sigh, he flipped the channel trying to find something to take his mind off this morning.

The smell of lavender filled the air and he groaned.

"Travis," she said with a smile, appearing before him. "I saw what happened this morning. Thank God you were there to save Samantha."

With a sigh, he feared where this conversation was going to go.

"She's safe," he said, wishing the ghost would disappear.

"How did it feel to hold a woman in your arms after all these years," she asked.

Glancing up at her, he wondered if using the same tactics he'd used to quiet Desiree would work. But Eugenia was his great-great-great-great-grandmother. He couldn't embarrass her, could he?

The memory of the bucket of mop water being dropped on him came to mind. Oh yes, maybe she needed to be embarrassed. Maybe then she would leave him alone.

"Do you really want to know?" he asked her.

"Of course, dear, I care about you and her," she said.

"When I saw how visibly shaken she was, I pulled her into my arms and held her close. I could feel her breasts crushed against my chest and she smelled of a light flowery fragrance. She felt wonderful in my arms and my pants…"

He couldn't say it.

"Travis Aaron Burnett, do not go there with me," she said.

"Well, you asked and wanted to know how she felt in my arms. I saved her from a rattlesnake. It's over. She's fine and I'm still going to remain alone."

For a moment, Eugenia just shimmered before him and he wanted her to leave him alone. Maybe they should call a ghost intervention. Send her back to the grave. He turned his attention to the television, hoping she'd get the message.

"The way I brought my son Travis together with Rose was to tell him she took my wedding ring. He wanted to believe the worst about her and I knew she was innocent. Maybe I should do that for you and Samantha."

"Sorry, won't work," he said.

"That will work, Travis. You should not be going through life alone. I want more grandbabies," she said. "Family members."

"Grandbabies? That's why you're tormenting me?"

"It's not torment. It's my way of trying to get you to pay attention to a beautiful woman who would be perfect for you. She's lonely. You're lonely. And the two of you look so cute together. You need to give love another chance. Take her out just once and I'll move on to Tanner," she said.

That was tempting. If he took her out riding, maybe Eugenia would leave him alone. That boy had yet to experience love, and Travis did believe that everyone should experience happiness at least once. But his chance had come and gone

"If I take her out riding or doing something, then you'll give up on pestering me?"

"I'll do my best," she said.

"Not good enough. You have to agree to leave me alone, and if you don't, then I'm going to call a spirit remover and have you removed from the premises."

"You wouldn't," she said.

"Oh, yes, I would. You haven't been speaking to the

guests, have you? None of them have run out of the cabins screaming yet."

There was silence for a moment.

"Eugenia?"

"They don't believe in me," she said. "Only the family knows who I am and even most of them don't acknowledge that they've seen me. Tanner refuses to believe. Tucker, he's not afraid of me. You're the only one who truly speaks to me and that's because I keep coming to see you."

Travis knew the woman's history. He knew that she liked to matchmake people. And now that he knew she wanted more grandchildren, he understood why she was here.

"Here's the deal. I am never going to remarry. Amanda was the love of my life and she will always be my only love. But if you will leave me alone, I'll take Samantha out once. Then it will be over."

A big smile spread across her face.

"You have to give her a chance," she said. "It can't be that you're just doing this to make me go away and leave you alone. Because I won't leave if that's what you're doing."

Would it hurt to give the woman a chance? He loved Amanda and always would, but he did get lonely. But another woman would never take her place. He would do what Eugenia asked, but he would remain alone and never marry again.

"All right, I'll ask her to go riding with me. But don't expect anything else. I'm not going to fall in love with her, marry her, or have the grandbabies you want. Do you understand me?"

The woman gave him a smile. "Of course, dear. All I'm asking of you is that you take a chance on her."

"And I'm asking you to go away and leave me alone after I go out with her. Go bother Tanner."

As she began to dissipate, she laughed. "He's not ready. But you are."

After she was gone, he shook his head. "The hell, I am."

CHAPTER 10

Tanner Burnett walked up beside Desiree in the recreation center where she was busy cleaning up the breakfast dishes and grinned. "Did you see what happened yesterday when Travis and Samantha were in the hen house and he killed that large rattler?"

"No," Desiree said, gazing at her cousin as she wiped down a table.

"Travis hugged Samantha. And I don't mean a polite simple hug. Oh no. He hugged her close and long and the way a man does when he likes a woman," he said.

Her eyes widened and she smiled. "Do you think he's interested in her? Every time we have guests, we try to push him with someone, but nothing happens. He ignores all the single ladies."

It was true. They had tried on more than one occasion to place a beautiful woman in his path, but he just ignored the lady. It was like he had blinders on, and yet with Samantha, he had responded differently.

"Don't know, but I say we give them a little help. He's always good about helping you whenever you need help cleaning cabins. I say you let him help you clean the cabins today."

She grinned and reached her fingers to her head. "I think I feel a migraine coming on."

"Which cabin is she staying in?"

"Number five," Tanner said.

"Oh dear," Desiree said.

The look on her face had him shaking his head. Why was his family so obsessed with the thought of a spirit from the past? It was nonsense.

"Don't give me that ghost bullshit," Tanner said. "I don't believe in it."

The woman giggled. "Believe whatever you want. But none of the hired help likes to clean cabin five and usually I do it. Today, I think Travis is going to get to clean cabin five."

After she had wiped the last table, they turned and walked across the yard, heading toward the barn where Travis was cleaning the stalls.

"Amanda has been gone for almost three years. It would be wonderful if he was to find someone," Desiree said. "But he loved her for so long, it would be weird to think of him with someone else."

Tanner nodded. He had been in Iraq and unable to attend the funeral, but he had always liked the woman his brother was crazy in love with. "Amanda would want him to be happy."

"Just like we all want *you* to be happy," Desiree said,

gazing at him.

Right now, he felt better than ever. The dreams and the battle scenes didn't seem to overwhelm him as much. The doctor had promised him that with time, he would get better, but that he would always risk having an episode.

For that reason, he would never marry.

With a shrug, he glanced around the ranch. "I am happy. I'm home. I'm not in a war zone. Believe me, nothing could make me any happier."

Just then one of the tractors backfired, and he grabbed Desiree, threw her to the ground, and covered her. The old survival instincts kicked in, filling his brain with adrenalin and fear.

"We're safe," Desiree said slowly and calmly. "It's all right."

With a sigh, he let her go and willed the terror inside him to go away. How long was it going to take him to get over being shot at? Or would he ever? There were people who never recovered. The doctor kept telling him to just give it time. It had been well over a year. How much more time did he need?

"Sorry," he said. "Some noises make me think I'm back in the sand taking cover."

She reached out and rubbed his arm.

"All right, I'm going to find Travis and tell him I have a severe migraine and the girls are too busy with the other cabins. Could he please clean cabin five?"

Tanner smiled and Desiree giggled. "We're acting like our great-great-great-great-grandmother."

"Don't start telling me we're playing matchmaker. We're just giving the chance of love a little help," he told her.

"Wait a minute," Desiree said suddenly frowning. "What do we know about this girl? Travis deserves someone special. His heart couldn't take getting hurt again."

It was true. He could see that his brother would be crushed if he did give her a chance and then learned there was something in her present or even past that was undesirable. But, then, Tucker said he thought he knew her.

"Tucker was going to find out about her. He thought he recognized her. She seems nice," Tanner said. "But then again, what do I know about women? I haven't gone on a date in seven years. Five in the military and then two years home."

Desiree stopped and gazed at him. "You need to change that. You need to get laid."

He started laughing. "What's that? The last time that happened I think I was in college."

"Time to change that. Even if it's just a friends-with-benefits," she said. "All right, I have to find Travis and I'll wait to learn what Tucker finds out about Mrs. Samantha Rollins."

Desiree turned and walked toward where Travis was in the barn. The thought of sleeping with a woman rolled around in his head. It had been a long time. Too long and he even wondered if he would remember.

Was it just like riding a bike?

Shaking his head, the thought seemed to grow on him. He didn't like picking women up in bars, but then again, there weren't too many around here. But in two weeks, he had to go to Dallas to the VA Hospital.

Maybe on the way home, he'd make a stop somewhere. Sometimes he liked to spend the night at a hotel. This might be the time to find someone and have a quick fling. Nothing permanent, just someone to knock the dust off.

With a smile, he walked toward the chuck wagon. He was going to get it ready for the big barbeque they were going to host after the rodeo.

Time to go to work.

But he had a plan. Sex in two weeks.

CHAPTER 11

Travis was in the barn when Desiree came to him, her face looked white and her green eyes seemed almost droopy.

"What's wrong with you?" he said, rubbing down one of the mares. The horse had been limping and he was checking to make certain she was all right. Anything to keep from facing his fear of asking Samantha to go out with him.

All morning, he'd been questioning why he'd agreed to Eugenia's terms last night. All morning, he had tried to figure out how to get out of spending time with Samantha and yet he also wanted to see her again. He was torn.

"Migraine. The girls are all busy. All I lack is cabin five. Could you please clean that one for me? I need to go rest."

Cabin five was Samantha's cabin. A frown appeared between his brows. They wouldn't be trying to put him and Samantha together would they? All he needed was additional family members to try what his matchmaking great-grandmother was doing.

Yet holding Samantha in his arms yesterday, comforting her, had felt good. Too good. It was like she fit right there and he'd wanted to continue holding her. He wanted to continue the pleasure he'd experienced of her fitting so perfectly against his body.

Plus, he'd promised Eugenia to take Samantha on one date. This could be a good time to ask her out. The thought left him nervous. He'd been in high school the last time he asked a woman on a date.

"Sure," he said. "Just as long as you promise me you're not trying to put us together."

Her brows raised and she glanced at him. "What? Who is in cabin five?"

Well, that made it sound like he was a crazy man. And after last night, maybe he was certifiably nuts.

"Never mind," he said. "You know I'm never getting involved with a woman again."

"So you've said many times." She shook her head. "You're young. Amanda is gone. Someday, I hope you move on, but it has to be in your time, no one else's. And my head hurts too bad to be able to think about convincing you to date."

"The only ladies in my life are these horses," he said.

With a sigh, she turned. "Thanks for taking care of the cabin. I'm going to lie down for a while."

Was she really feeling that bad?

"Hey, have you seen Tanner?"

"He's working in the chuck wagon," she said and walked out the door.

Well, she did know where his brother was. Could they have talked? Yesterday afternoon, Tanner had gone out of his way to tell him that Samantha looked really good in his arms. He didn't need his family trying to find him a woman. He had Eugenia driving him mad. Their combined forces working together would send him running.

Not even a woman as beautiful as Samantha would have him reconsidering his desire to be unfaithful to his dead wife. He would ask Samantha out and that would be the end of it.

When he finished with the horses, he stepped outside the barn and there was Desiree's utility cart waiting for him.

Pushing it along, he felt like a fool. Not because usually one of the girls did this, but because he was eager to see Samantha again. Last night, she had been missing when they sat around the campfire and made s'mores.

Today was a leisure day where they could go to the recreation center and play games or do arts and crafts. But he wasn't in charge of those activities. Those were Desiree's.

When he reached her cabin, he pulled his shirt straight and smelled his breath. What in the hell was he doing? He wasn't sixteen any longer.

His fist rapped on the cabin door. "Housekeeping."

Samantha opened up and stepped out on the porch, closing the barrier behind her. What was she doing that she didn't want him to see inside?

"Good morning," she said.

"Good morning," he replied. "I'm your maid today. Desiree is not feeling very well and I brought you fresh towels and linens. If you'll let me in, I'll hang them up and make the bed."

"That's very kind of you," she said. "The bed is made. All I need is towels. Nothing else. The cabin doesn't need cleaning."

That was odd. Most people wanted them to do everything including clean the toilets. He wasn't going to complain, but it was odd that she didn't want to let him in. Was she hiding something?

"Are you doing all right," he asked her. "I know you were pretty scared by that snake yesterday."

She leaned back against the door and gazed up at him, smiling, and his heart skipped a beat. "I hate snakes. But I'm fine. Don't expect me to collect the eggs for you anymore this week. That's a job for someone else."

Nervously, he licked his lips. For his own sanity, he had to do Eugenia's bidding. He had to ask Samantha out. And yet, staring at her wasn't a chore or an obligation; he wanted to spend more time with this woman.

No one had interested him since the death of Amanda. And yet Samantha was intriguing. He wanted to know more about who she was.

"Would you like to go horseback riding this afternoon? Or a hike in the woods?"

She licked her lips nervously. Her eyes seem to brighten and yet she wasn't jumping at the chance. The first time he had invited a woman to do something with him and she was going to turn him down.

The smell of lavender drifted on the breeze and fear seized Travis.

Eugenia.

That damn ghost was about to make an appearance and he had to keep Samantha from seeing her. If she'd been afraid of the snake, she'd be terrified of seeing someone who lived over a hundred years ago appear.

The sparkles announcing her appearance shimmered at the side of Samantha.

Oh no. What was he going to do to keep Samantha from seeing his dead ancestor?

Taking a step toward her, he grabbed her and did the only thing he could think of at the moment. His lips came down on hers and he kissed her while the smell of lavender surrounded them.

At first, he was tender, but then a fierceness overcame him, and it was like the flood gates of desire swamped him, filling him as he took command and his lips overpowered hers. An explosion of yearning rattled him as his mouth moved over hers, his tongue delved inside her mouth.

She tasted of coffee and donuts and it was all he could do to keep from slamming her against the door and pressing his hard cock against her.

Even though he'd kissed her to keep her from seeing Eugenia, he didn't want to let go. He didn't want to release her and have her step out of his arms. He didn't want to hear her tell him no when he so desperately needed her to say yes.

In the background, he heard laughter, and the smell of lavender slowly dissipated. Eugenia had been laughing at him trying to keep Samantha from seeing her. Putting everything into kissing Samantha to keep her from seeing the ghost.

Knowing the kiss had gotten out of hand, he suddenly pulled back.

"Sorry, it's just…you're the first woman I've kissed in almost three years and I got a little carried away."

She was holding her fingers up to her mouth. It was red. Her lips were swollen from his kiss and he had to control the urge to kiss her again.

"Yes, I'll go for a horseback ride with you," she said, gazing at him like she was dumbfounded.

"I promise not to kiss you," he said, guilt filling him.

Frowning at him, she shook her head. "Like hell. Then I'm not going," she said. "I kind of liked that kiss. It made my brains leak from my ears."

A ripple of desire spiraled through him. It was the first time he'd felt that way since Amanda died.

"Your brains leaked from your ears?"

"It's a saying, and well, yes, I liked your kiss."

A grin spread across his face and he chuckled. "Yeah, I kind of liked it too."

He lifted his hat and ran his hand through his hair then plopped it back on his head.

His cousins teased him, saying that whenever he did that, he was thinking too much. And right now he was thinking of how he'd like to push her into her room and let their bodies explore whatever else they liked.

He had to put some distance between them and a bed.

"Meet me at the barn in thirty minutes."

"All right," she said and went to step back inside.

Suddenly he remembered this was supposed to be a date. A chance to get to know each other a little more without the prying ears and eyes of his family.

He jerked to a halt. "Have you eaten today?"

"No," she said with a grin. "I've been working."

She was supposed to be on vacation. What had she been working on? What did she even do for a living?

"I'll get us a picnic lunch," he said. "Give me forty-five minutes."

She grinned at him and it was all he could do to keep from grabbing her again. That smile lit a fire within him. One he had to run from or get singed.

"See you soon," she said and stepped back into the room and closed the door.

What the hell had he just done? He'd made a date with a woman he was really attracted to. But Amanda…he'd made a promise to her that she would be his only love for the rest of his life.

How could he break that promise?

CHAPTER 12

What the hell was Samantha doing? She sat on the sorrel mare and kicked the sides as she and Travis galloped down the road. It was a gorgeous spring day, and she'd pulled out her cowboy hat from the days she had attended school here.

What made her decide to bring it, she didn't know, but now she was glad.

When they were away from prying eyes, he glanced over at her and grinned.

"You were hiding how well you ride the other day," he said.

She shrugged. "I was with a bunch of greenhorns and didn't want to make them look bad."

"I'm glad you're a good rider. We can go farther and I won't have to worry about you so much," he said.

"Maybe I want you to worry about me," she said laughing.

"Yesterday was enough of a scare for me," he said.

And she couldn't disagree. That damn snake had frightened her. She'd forgotten how scary rattlers could be. And yet she had enjoyed the feeling of being in his arms way too much. Just like she'd enjoyed his kiss this morning.

"So you haven't kissed anyone in a long time. Why not?" she asked.

"We'll play truth or dare when we reach the creek," he said. "Until then, eyes on the trail and not on me."

"Well, damn, that won't be any fun," she replied, knowing he was probably right, but she was anxious to learn why this man was alone. She knew the reason she had no one, but what made him a loner?

A grove of trees was in the distance and she hoped that's where they were going.

"Like the hat," he said.

"Good, I've had it since I was a kid," she replied, thinking of how she loved this hat because her daddy had purchased it for her. It had been his last gift to her before he died.

The horses picked up speed.

"They know there is a watering hole up ahead," he said. "And, yes, there are water moccasins in the river, so don't go near it without me being close."

Water moccasins were nasty little creatures who liked to steal your bait when you fished in the river or your fish on a stringer if you gave them half a chance. The thought of them brought back memories of fishing with her father.

"I've had enough snake adventures for a lifetime," she said, knowing that soon she needed to drive to the cemetery. But she had spent so much time with Eugenia that she didn't like to leave the cabin.

He glanced at her and grinned.

"Why aren't you working in a big city," she asked, thinking he would look great in a suit and tie.

"Uh-huh," he said. "Look at the scenery, look out for your horse. I'm not answering anything until we get to where we're going."

Shaking her head, she had so many questions for him, but none he was going to answer until they were off these horses.

She reached down and ran her hand along the silky mane of the beautiful animal she was riding. She'd forgotten how much she enjoyed this.

"You're not a serial killer who is luring me out into the woods, are you? I must warn you that I took self-defense and I'm a mean woman you don't want to mess with."

Laughing, he glanced at her and shook his head. "I kill Cheerios every morning. A little milk, a little sugar or a banana, and those natural grains don't stand a chance."

She grinned. "I'm a Lucky Charms killer myself."

Why did she enjoy this man's company? It was the first time in the three years since her divorce that she'd felt at ease with a man. With others, he came off a little grumpy, but with her, they laughed and smiled, and now he'd kissed her. And she couldn't wait until he did it again.

"How did you get out of doing dude ranch duties today?"

"We take turns, and this afternoon is arts and crafts with Desiree," he said frowning. "Of course, she has a migraine, so I don't know who will do her session this afternoon."

Samantha would have to check on her later today.

They entered a canopy of trees and the hot sun disappeared. Their horses walked up to the river and began to drink. She watched as Travis glanced around.

"Checking for snakes," he said.

Good, because she did not want to see another one as close as she had seen the last one.

"Looks safe," he said, swinging his leg over his horse and dropping to the ground.

He came over to her and after she swung her leg over, he placed his hands on her waist and helped her alight.

God, his hands felt so good. Strong and rugged and the image of those big hands skimming down her naked skin had her gazing into his dark emerald eyes as her breath caught in her throat.

She licked her lips and tried to think of anything besides sex. It had been forever, and she couldn't remember what it felt like to desire a man. That had ended years ago.

"I had the kitchen make us a picnic basket. Our old cook is retiring next week and we have a new woman coming in from Boulder, Colorado."

"Nice," she said, not knowing what else to say. For the first time, she felt nervous. Was this a date? They lived thousands of miles apart and whatever this was between them could go nowhere. Especially if he learned she was recording Eugenia. What was she doing taking a chance with Travis?

And yet, it felt good. It felt right and she didn't want to think about what would happen if he ever knew the truth about her.

He took out a blanket and spread it over the ground. She stood watching him. Fear seemed to have frozen her in place. What would he think if she jumped back on her horse and returned to the ranch?

Her first date in three years and it was with a billionaire cowboy on a dude ranch in Texas. How crazy was that? At least she knew it could go nowhere, so this was her chance to practice her dating skills, which were rusty.

Who was she kidding? She didn't want to sharpen her dating skills. All she wanted was a chance to spend time with Travis and learn more about the ranch. Nothing else.

And yet, as she gazed at him, she could feel her womanly bits crying out in surrender. *Take me! Take me! Take me!*

Never going to happen.

Sinking onto the ground, he looked back at her. "Are you going to join me?"

"Yes, I was just plotting my escape," she said in a smart-aleck way to cover her anxiety. She feared that if he touched her, she would go up in flames.

"Am I that terrifying?"

She sat on the blanket. "Yes and no. You're the first date I've had in three years."

A grin spread across his face. "It's been even longer for me. Wonder what else we have in common? You said you're not good at marriage. Why?"

Lying back on her elbows, she gazed up at him. "I put

my career first instead of my husband. It's so important to me that I be successful and he got tired of always being last. I came home early one evening to surprise him and caught him and a woman in bed together."

The memory of that evening still hurt and yet she was better off without Dewayne.

"Cheating is never the answer," he said.

"No, but I wasn't a good wife and he let me know that."

Before the final hearing on her divorce, he'd let her know exactly why he'd cheated on her. And that this wasn't the first time. Only the time he got caught.

"I know you're in television, but what do you do?"

"I'm a producer." It wasn't a complete lie. Just not the full truth. "Right now, I'm working on a new season that we'll start production on as soon as I get back."

"Which show?"

Dear God, how did she get out of this? "It's on one of the smaller cable channels. Buyer beware. It's about houses."

She had totally lied. And she hated lying to anyone, but she couldn't tell him the right answer or he would be walking her off the property. And she wasn't ready to go.

He pulled out some canned drinks and bottled water. She took the water. No need for extra calories.

"What about you? Why is this your first date?"

He sighed and she could see his mind working to tell her, but she got the feeling he didn't want to talk about his past.

"Similar situation. She's gone and I'm alone," he said, looking off in the distance. "I'm good at marriage. I'm good at relationships, but after the last one, I decided I was done."

"Me too," she said, gazing at him. "I've not met anyone. I've buried myself in my work and you're the first man who's…"

Oh crap, how did she get out of telling him that he was the first man to awaken her body since college when she met Dewayne?

"I'm the first man who's done what?"

He wasn't going to let it go.

"Let's just say that kiss awakened parts of me that I'd long forgotten about. My libido was doing the mamba and saying *She's alive. She's alive.*"

Lying back on the blanket, he chuckled. His laugh was deep and then he rolled over and faced her.

"So here we are, two lonely people who have been burned by love and now we're just trying to get through life without getting involved and hurt again."

She thought about what he'd said for a moment and realized it was true.

"You got it," she said. "I'm not interested in marriage or love or a happily ever after. After Dewayne, I don't believe in them anymore."

Now her work was her interest. And yet, gazing at Travis, she was having second thoughts.

Travis nodded. "And I had it all, but now it's gone, and I don't believe I can ever get so lucky again. It sounds like we're in agreement."

"Yes," she said. "So let's have a fling this week and then

on Saturday, I fly home to New York and you can return to being the grump that everyone believes you to be."

Stupefied, she was shocked at what had come out of her mouth. She'd never had a fling in her life. Dewayne had been her first and she had planned on being married to him forever. But this seemed right. It felt like what they both needed.

A grin spread across his face. "So tell me what a *fling* entails."

"Kissing," she said, not knowing what else to say.

"Sex?"

A grin spread across her face. She had not had sex since her divorce. She wasn't into one-night stands. She didn't believe in spreading her legs for just every man out there.

"Wouldn't you like that? It's been almost four years since I've had sex, so I don't know if I remember how. Let's just see where this goes."

She wasn't ready to promise him the moon.

And she knew it was not going anywhere because she would get on that plane and return to New York, show her boss hole the footage she had and get on with her life.

And he would hate her once the Burnett family learned what she'd done.

No man was going to distract her from her goals. She planned on being the next big woman in television. Her ghost hunting show was going to be the hottest thing ever once they saw the evidence of Eugenia. And Travis would be furious once he learned of her deception.

Travis rolled over and was suddenly on top of her and she gazed up into his emerald eyes.

"You make me feel alive. For almost three years, I've felt dead inside and suddenly I have the stirrings of desire. I'm not giving up on having sex with you just yet. But I understand that your priorities are your career. I refuse to be a one-night fling."

A smile spread across her face. She liked the idea of it not being one night as well. There was so much about Travis that she liked.

She liked the way he felt on top of her. She could feel his hardness pressing into the V of her legs. Already, her heart was flittering and she could feel her body opening, ready to receive him.

But there were secrets between them. Secrets that would destroy the chance of them ever coming together permanently.

"Don't give up. In fact, kiss me. Show me how much you want me. But I'll just tell you, it's not happening today. I'm not ready. But I do desire you."

And she wasn't. In fact, the thought terrified her. It had been so long, she'd stopped shaving her lady bits.

A grin spread across his face. "Good."

His lips covered hers and she let herself sink into the feelings that he evoked. Damn, this was so good, and yet, she knew he would not appreciate what she had hidden.

But she didn't want to stop him as he explored her mouth. How long had it been since a man made her feel this way? Too long. Way too long.

CHAPTER 13

When Travis returned to his home that afternoon, he felt torn. They had spent the afternoon on the blanket, kissing until both of their lips were swollen, their desire a raging beast between them. Oh, how he had wanted to take it to the next step, but when she told him she wasn't ready, he respected her decision.

And in many ways, he wasn't either. There had been no one since Amanda. Even now, he wasn't certain he wanted to take it to the next step with Samantha. Especially considering how Eugenia would react. He'd done his part of the deal and now she would go away and leave him alone.

But would she?

Damn, that didn't mean he couldn't dream about Samantha and how it would be, and that's when the guilt started in. The memory of Amanda's beautiful smiling face had him all torn up inside. He would always love her, miss her, and probably a small piece of him would forever mourn her. They had been together since they were both sixteen. There had never been anyone else.

Though, he was a man, and a man had needs. Samantha could so very easily fill those needs. Would this fling last more than a week? He didn't know. Right now he just wanted to enjoy the moment. To feel her full breasts pressed against his chest once again, to kiss her until they were both delirious with need. To cup her buttocks and pull her in even closer.

Just thinking about her, his cock was hard and his heart was pounding. It would not do for him to get serious about her because she admitted her career came first and that would never do for Travis.

That's why he thought this little fling would be good for both of them. Get this itch taken care of and then he could go another three years without a woman. At least, he hoped he could. But Samantha was unique.

With a sigh, he sank down on his couch and gazed at the home he'd built after Amanda's death. This was his sanctuary, and while he loved living here alone, sometimes he felt like the walls were closing in. Sometimes he wanted to run out into the yard and scream *why did you leave me?*

But that would be a waste of time and energy. And they would probably haul him off on a stretcher pumped full of drugs that would help him forget he was losing his mind.

His cell phone rang and he glanced down at the number. Tucker.

"Hey," he said. "How's LA?"

"Deplorable," Tucker said. "If I didn't make so much money, I'd never come back here."

It was one of the reasons that Travis never left Texas. This was home.

"Then get your ass home," he said.

"I wish, but my starlet is performing tonight and I have the entire crew here to keep her safe."

His brother protected beautiful music stars and even some actresses, and he took his job very seriously.

"Sounds like you're busy," Travis said, wondering why he'd called.

"Very, but I had to call you and tell you about one of your guests. Samantha Rollins. I knew I had seen her face before. Her maiden name is Samantha Griffin. She attended our elementary school before her family moved away. Her father was Jimmy Griffin, the professional bull rider who lived not far away. He died when she was eight or nine."

The news seemed like he'd had a dose of cold water splashed on him. Why the hell had she not told him who she was? They knew the same people. Grew up in the same small town. Went to the same schools.

He remembered her father's funeral and seeing her standing by his grave, gazing down with a lost expression on her face.

"The kids used to bully her, and if I remember, one year when the school came for a cookout, they chased her, calling her carrot top."

Dear God, he remembered. She'd run away and hid and the sponsors had spent at least an hour searching for her.

When they found her, she demanded that they call her mother. And she went home. It was the last time he'd ever seen her. Until now.

"You're sure this is her because she didn't mention it to me and we've grown close," Travis said, feeling hurt that she would keep the information from him. Hell, his tongue had been down her throat today, his hand caressed her breast and he'd wanted to…She could have said something.

"I'm sending you the pictures I found of her. She looks a hell of a lot different than she did as a kid, but I'm certain this is her."

"Well, shit," Travis said, his anger spilling over. He'd almost slept with her and she hadn't been honest about who she was. Why not? What was she hiding?

Why would she not tell him she lived here.

"Anyway, I gotta run, but I thought you should know."

"Why would she keep this a secret?"

"Don't know. You should ask her," Tucker said.

"Believe me, I will. She has some explaining to do."

"Be careful," Tucker said. "Showtime. I've got to run."

There was a click and the phone went dead. With a sigh, Travis sank back against the couch. Was she trying to get even for the children being so mean to her by taking it out on the Burnetts?

Travis scrolled through his phone and saw the pictures that Tucker sent him. She didn't even look like the same person. The woman he spent the afternoon kissing was gorgeous and this poor kid had been harassed so badly in school. Bullied, to be exact.

Carrot top. That had been the name they called her.

As he scrolled, he came across a picture of Amanda and his chest ached. Why had she been taken from him? Why was he once again in the dating pool he'd never wanted to experience?

Eugenia.

Well, he'd upheld his part of the bargain. Now it was time for her to go. He was done.

With a sigh, he glanced at the clock and knew it was time to head to the recreation room where supper would be served.

Time to let Samantha know her secret was out.

Time for Mrs. Griffin-Rollins to be revealed.

CHAPTER 14

When Samantha reached the cabin, she'd half expected Eugenia to reveal herself, but the meter was silent. No ghosts were here, just her and the memory of how she'd spent the afternoon kissing Travis like they were school kids.

Her lips were swollen, her body ached in places she'd forgotten about and it was all she could do not to call him up and say come to her cabin. But that could never happen because then he would learn the truth.

And yet, it was eating at her that she was keeping a very large secret from a man she felt attracted to. The first man in years that she was drawn to and she was not being honest with him. First, he didn't know who she really was, and second, he had no idea that she was a ghost hunter with her own show.

And she'd lied about her job, her show, everything. The man didn't realize that they knew each other as children.

There were so many lies between them that she didn't think they could ever be together.

With a sigh, she sank down on the bed and glanced about the room. She'd been so young when Eugenia had comforted her that first time. She had been sitting on the floor crying her eyes out, wishing that she was beautiful and that the other kids accepted her, liked her. How sad for a child not to be liked.

But Eugenia was the one who told her none of that mattered because she would one day grow up to be a swan. A beautiful swan that the other girls would be envious of. And she had.

Though she had been in college when she finally realized that carrot top was now one of the most beautiful girls on campus. That men wanted to date her.

She had been invited to join a beauty contest and won. That's when her journalism teacher took notice of her and told her she could make it in television.

If this thing with Travis went much further, she would have to be honest with him and then he would hate her. And yet, she wouldn't give up her career for any man. Though she'd lost at love once before because of her desire for a great career, she didn't want to fail again. At either her career or marriage. Maybe she wasn't one of those women who could have it all. Maybe she just needed to work on her career and forget about love and even marriage.

Glancing at the clock, she realized it was time to eat dinner in the recreation center. Her heart did a little *cathunk* at the thought of seeing Travis. As much as she was trying to deny the desire she felt when she saw him, she was eager to spend more time alone with him.

Rising from the bed, she quickly changed into a lightweight summer dress and sandals. Knowing it would be dark when she returned, she grabbed her flashlight and her phone and locked the cabin door behind her with the do-not-disturb sign swinging from the doorknob.

So far, she'd kept the maids out. She wanted that to continue. If they found her equipment, she would be told to leave.

As she walked toward the recreation center, the sun was slowly sinking below the horizon. A cool breeze blew and a sense of anticipation filled her.

Country music could be heard and she wondered if tonight was the dance. She had forgotten to look at the schedule after spending the day with Travis.

As she stepped onto the outside deck, she stopped and breathed the fresh air. There were so many things about Texas that she'd forgotten. So many things about this area that she loved.

Walking inside, she glanced around and didn't see Travis.

Inside, Mr. Stephens grabbed her. "Let's dance."

He swirled her out onto the dance floor and she couldn't help but freeze up. This was not who she wanted to spend the evening with. When the music ended, she smiled at him.

"Thank you, I'm going to go eat," she said and walked away shaking her head.

Some men were just known predators and she feared that about Mr. Stephens.

Glancing around, she did not see Travis, but went ahead and filled her plate with barbecue, avoiding the snake. A shiver rippled through her at the thought of that ugly python staring at her.

When her plate was full, she found a seat at the table with an older couple, the Langfords.

"May I join you?"

"Yes, please," the older woman said. "Are you having a good time?"

"Of course," she said. "I went horseback riding with Travis today. We rode down to the creek. It was beautiful. What about you guys?"

The older couple glanced at one another and laughed. "I learned how to make a napkin holder while Joe napped."

"Damn good nap too," the older man said.

The couple was entertaining and she loved how even now they would glance at one another and you could see the happiness, the caring, they shared between them.

Just then she saw Travis walk in the door. His jeans were pressed and creased perfectly, with a big shiny buckle. His plaid cowboy shirt clung to his muscles and he had on a white hat, polished boots, and probably smelled delicious. And she wanted to fling herself in his arms and lick every inch of him.

She waved to him and he nodded, but he didn't seem in a hurry to reach her. After this afternoon, she would have thought he would have come to her side first. But he didn't.

Turning, he walked over to the food and got in line. By now, her plate was mostly empty and she pushed it aside.

The band continued to play, but the music wasn't loud and pounding like in a club. It was quiet background noise. Some couples were up on the dance floor dancing and she wished that Travis would waltz with her.

After he filled his plate, he joined his cousins at a family table. For a second, she felt hurt, and then she realized that maybe he couldn't fraternize with the guests. She continued to sit with the older couple, trying not to feel slighted, but it was hard.

Finally, after he'd thrown away his plate, he walked over to her.

"Would you like to dance?"

"Yes," she said, hopeful once again. When had this man's attention become so important to her? Why did her body seem to hum with pleasure when he walked up beside her?

He pulled her into his arms and they began to waltz around the floor.

"Tucker called me about you this afternoon," he said, gazing into her eyes.

"Oh?" she said, wondering what his brother who was into security had learned about her.

People danced past them and Travis slowed his steps. His hand gently held hers as his other hand guided her around the dance floor.

"He remembered who you were and even sent me some pictures of you," he said. "Why didn't you tell me you were Samantha Griffin?"

Was that all he told him? Had he not learned that she was Samantha Rollins host of *Ghost Seekers*?

"Because as a child I was never treated well here. In school, the girls called me carrot top and loved to make fun of me. Why would I want people to remember me that way?"

Shaking his head, he stared at her. "But you're beautiful. If you felt that way, why would you return?"

Now that was a much harder question to answer without giving away the real reason. So she went for his sympathy.

"My father died here. I've never had good memories of this part of Texas and I decided to see if I could change that. And until this moment, I was doing well. But somehow I get the feeling you're angry with me."

The music came to an end and people walked around them off the dance floor.

A frown appeared on his face and his emerald eyes darkened. "I guess I am. I expected you to be honest with me."

No, she couldn't be honest, or else he would tell her to leave. As much as she hated lying to him, she could not tell him the truth.

"Why? I was here as Samantha Rollins to make new memories. Only you changed things, and this afternoon when I returned to my cabin, I wondered if I should tell you the truth. While I rested, I lay there on the bed, trying to decide when to tell you. Should I wait until right before I left or tell you now?"

Oh, if only he knew how there was so much more about

her that he would definitely not like. But she wasn't going to tell him that part. At least not yet.

"I don't understand why you weren't honest."

The man had no concept of what it felt like to return to a place where you didn't feel wanted or accepted.

"Have you ever been bullied in your life? Do you know what it's like when all the girls in school turn on you? And then your father dies in a horrible accident and your world is completely turned upside down? Your mother yanks you away from everything you've ever known and moves you clear across the country. That year was not my best year."

They stood there in the middle of the dance floor staring at one another.

"No one picked on the Burnett kids because there were so many of us," he said softly.

"I'm sure they didn't," she said, thinking of how she had wanted brothers and sisters, but her mother had told her it would never happen. "When you're alone and you have crooked teeth, carrot-colored hair, and speech impediments, they treat you like you're a leper. And if you don't remember, I'm sure someone in your family does."

The music began to play again and she turned and walked away from Travis. If he couldn't understand, maybe it was better that she ended this now. After all, she had other secrets he had yet to discover.

Secrets that would destroy them.

Suddenly she felt his hand on her arm. "Do you remember Amanda Dixon?"

"Yes," she said. "She was one of the few who were nice to me."

"I married her when we were both eighteen."

Oh my God, she had been kissing a married man. What was she doing? She just needed to leave men alone.

"Where is she?"

"She died almost three years ago," he said and turned and walked away.

Son of a bitch. First, he confronts her about her identity and then he tells her about his wife and walks away, leaving her standing on the dance floor.

Oh no, he wasn't going to get away with that. Yes, she hadn't told him her secrets, but he'd kept some of his own.

Walking up behind him, she whirled him around. "I'm sorry about your wife. That's why you haven't been with a woman in three years."

"That's correct. She would not have lied about her identity."

She hadn't exactly lied about her identity.

"Whoa, wait just a minute. I never lied. I reserved the cabin in my married name. You're just mad because I didn't stop you and say 'hey remember me? I'm the girl they called carrot top in school. The one who after being tormented ran and hid.' You're mad because your brother recognized me and you didn't."

People were beginning to watch them.

He grabbed her by the hand and pulled her out the door where they walked away from the recreation center. The moon was glowing and the stars were shining. And instead of kissing or making out, they were arguing.

"Yes, I'm mad because you're the first woman I've let get this close to me. And I feel like you haven't been honest."

She shrugged. "So? You're the first man I've been this close to since my divorce three years ago. Did you tell me all your personal secrets? You haven't been honest with me."

"I don't have secrets," he said.

Without thinking, she threw back her head and laughed. "Really?"

"I'm a Burnett who has lived here all my life. What else do you need to know?"

"How did your wife die?"

"I don't talk about that," he said, and she could see the dawning of understanding on his face.

Slowly he was starting to realize that he was keeping secrets from her as well. She wasn't the only one who hadn't been completely honest.

"I don't like to relive my childhood and tell everyone I meet that the kids called me carrot top and all other kinds of names."

With a sigh, he stared up at the moon. "Why are we fighting?"

It was such a startling question that she gasped and then it hit her full force.

"Because we don't trust one another," she said in a sad tone.

In fact, right now, she just wanted to pack her bags and ghost equipment and go home. Maybe she'd had enough that she didn't need any more.

Suddenly he grabbed her face and brought his lips to hers. He kissed her like a man who was starving, his mouth commanding her surrender. His tongue delving inside and stroking the inside of her mouth.

Like a limp doll, she leaned into him and experienced his kiss, her blood heating, her breath freezing in her lungs, her arms winding around his neck, pulling him in deeper.

This would never work. They could never be a couple, and yet, he felt so good and she needed him so badly. Maybe they could just use each other, but that would never work. She'd never done anything so scandalous in her life.

Finally, he released her mouth and glanced down into her eyes. She could see the mistrust still there. She knew that they were still not in a good place

"Damn, woman, I want you so bad and yet, you're right. Neither one of us trusts the other."

"And we're both not ready to surrender everything for the other."

"No," he said. "I had sworn off women and relationships after Amanda died."

"And I had sworn off men and relationships after my husband cheated on me."

They were neither one ready, yet Samantha knew this chemistry, or whatever it was between them, was potent and powerful, and the longer she stayed, the bigger the chance of them falling into bed together.

He shook his head. "Yet, you're the first woman since Amanda that I've wanted."

"And you're the first man I've wanted since Dewayne," she said with a telling gasp.

She stepped out of his arms, remembering her secret. "Nothing has to be decided right now."

"No, it doesn't."

She had to get away from him or find herself tucked in his bed, exploring his body. And that would not be good.

"Goodnight, Travis. Sweet dreams," she said and walked away.

Maybe she should walk away and never look back. Maybe she should leave before he learned the truth.

CHAPTER 15

Travis watched as Samantha walked away. His chest tightened as he thought of the young girl who had been bullied. She must've found it very hard to trust anyone. She must look at people and hope they never remember that girl and he understood why she refused to tell anyone.

And yet that made him distrustful and frustrated him even more that she had not told him the truth about who she was from day one.

In the same situation, what would he have done?

The band continued to play, but he had no desire to go back in and have to explain to his cousins what happened. So instead, he turned toward home.

It had been a long day and tomorrow was the rodeo. An event he helped coordinate and lead. But this week's guests were on the last half of their stay and he was ready for them to go home. All of them but Samantha.

There was something between them, but he wasn't certain what it was. Yet. But he wanted to find out.

His boots crunched on the ground as he headed to his home on the back of the property. When a Burnett turned twenty-one, they were given five acres to build a house on, and over the years, they had built a little community of homes.

The big grand house would someday be his, but until then, he lived in his small home. Walking up, he turned the doorknob and entered.

Silence.

Not the sound of Amanda's laughter or the cry of their child. Silence.

Walking over to the table, he set his hat down and then sank onto the couch to watch the news.

Suddenly the smell of lavender filled the air and a shimmery Eugenia appeared.

"What are you doing?" she asked.

"With regards to what?"

"Samantha. That poor girl suffered a lot as a child. Why are you so angry that she didn't tell you who she was? She has tried to put all that behind her and you made her relive it tonight."

Eugenia was dressed in a tight bodice with a full skirt and had an apron on. He'd heard many stories about her, but only recently had she begun to appear. At first, he'd been afraid, but he no longer feared her.

Though he did wish to hell she would go away and leave him alone. Why was he the lucky family member she liked to torment?

"Don't you think honesty and trust are important between a man and a woman?"

"Yes, but you have got to give her time. She has secrets. Things she has not told you and she must trust you before she can be honest with you."

That was odd. How did this ghost know of her secrets? How did she know that Samantha had to trust him before she told him said secrets? What were they hiding?

"How do you know she has secrets?"

"Everyone has secrets," the ghost replied.

Odd, wasn't that what Samantha said tonight. And then he'd told her a little about Amanda. Not enough that she knew what happened to her, but she knew his wife died.

"What are her secrets?"

The ghost shook her head. "Grandson, you've lost one wife. I'm doing my best to get you another wife, but you have to help me."

What in the hell was she talking about? He didn't need his great-great-great-great-grandmother's help.

"Hey, we made a deal and I held up my portion of the deal. I took Samantha horseback riding today. We spent the afternoon together. You said take her out just once and I did."

The ghost laughed. "And you did an excellent job. But, dear, I witnessed what you were doing on that blanket. I know there is a strong attraction between the two of you. Accept you're attracted to her, and I'll start working with Tanner. But you must continue to see Samantha."

The woman had watched them kissing on the blanket. Oh dear, that was creepy. What more did she want? He'd already done what she asked and now he wanted her to go away.

"I don't need your help," he said, wondering how a ghost thought she could play matchmaker.

"Of course, you do," she said. "Look at you. You're handsome, strong, a billionaire, whatever that is, and you help run this ranch. But you need a wife and babies so the ranch continues."

This was incredible. Sure, she had spoken to him before now, but she'd never told him her purpose and he truly believed the ghost thought this was what she was here to do. Play matchmaker and get them married.

"I did what you asked. Why are you still here?"

"Because my family needs me. This generation is in trouble. It needs my help. You need Samantha. She's a strong woman and would make you an excellent partner."

"Whoa, whoa, whoa," he said, glancing up at her like she was crazy, which she probably was. "I'm not getting married again. The house will be given to Tanner as a wedding gift, but I've had my chance at love."

The woman had the nerve to laugh. "You would have never made it in the old west. I married not once, but twice, and still outlived both my husbands. Your uncles fought wars, cattle rustlers, and gunslingers to get what they wanted. You lose your first wife and you're ready to quit. You don't recognize Samantha and you think she's lying to you. As you kids say, get over yourself."

Speechless, he sat there and stared at the woman who had started their family. Shaking his head, he had a crazy ghost telling him how he had failed.

"Amanda was the love of my life," he said.

"And Thomas Burnett was my first husband, but he died. And I went on," she said softly. "I married my true love the second time. Amanda would want you to go on. To find love again. To give love a chance. And no, it's not going to be easy. There are things both of you are not confessing yet. Samantha is right that there is no trust between you. Go build that trust."

With that, she suddenly dissipated leaving him all alone. If he was a drinking man, he would have thought he was drunk or had taken some kind of hallucinating drug. But he was as clean as a whistle.

How many other families had dead patriarchs who showed up to tell them how they were screwing things up? Or made them a promise and then didn't keep it?

"Only the Burnetts," he said out loud. "Maybe I need to see a shrink."

"She wouldn't help," a voice called that he recognized as Eugenia.

Travis bust out laughing. "Go do whatever ghosts do and leave me alone."

"No way," she called. "You're my grandson. Now listen to me. Go build trust with Samantha."

With a sigh, he turned on the television. Maybe there was something in the news that would get his mind off the things he'd lost and the things he wanted so desperately but was afraid to chance.

CHAPTER 16

*E*ugenia had not appeared in the last twenty-four hours, and Samantha was beginning to fear that she'd never see her again. Her time at the dude ranch was coming to a close and she only had three days to finish recording the outspoken ghost.

Today, she had decided she was not going to sit in the cabin waiting for her to show up. Today, she was going to avoid Travis. Today was going to be all about her and she had put on her bathing suit, found her latest book, and was now lying out by the pool getting some sun.

She'd swam for maybe ten minutes, and now she lay drying off, reading the latest ghost hunter novel about how to find paranormal activity and what to do when you locate the apparition. None of his ghosts acted like Eugenia. He told of the apparitions being mean and causing trouble, but Eugenia was sweet and kind and focused on her family.

"What are you reading," she heard from the voice that

always sent chills trickling down her spine. What about this man seemed to awaken all the nerves in her body that she thought were hibernating? Why did her lady parts awake to some island beat and start dancing the tango?

All she wanted to do was shout *go back into hibernation and stay there.*

"A book about paranormal activity," she said, not wanting to mention ghost hunting.

"Why? It's all a bunch of bunk," he said, sinking down onto the lounge chair next to her.

If only he knew the truth.

"It's something that fascinates me," she told him, wishing he would go away before he realized that she was the person from the ghost hunting show. Before he realized she was ghost hunting in cabin five.

"Why does it fascinate you?"

Most of the time, she loved it when someone asked her questions about the show and why she enjoyed ghost hunting, but not now. Not with Travis, because she feared he would figure out why she was here.

Still, he deserved to know a little about what drove her. There were parts of the tale she couldn't tell him.

"When I was a child, I had an experience with a ghost. It comforted me and brought me peace. Since then I've been trying to learn as much as I can about them. And I've been searching for that ghost."

And she'd found her right here in cabin five.

He frowned and shook his head.

"Are you certain it was a ghost? Have you ever seen one since?"

"Yes, to both questions," she said, wishing she could tell him about the ghost in cabin five, shocked that he didn't know one of his dead relatives was speaking to her. But she was not going to be the one to inform him that this ranch had paranormal activity. Lots of activity, and it all centered in her cabin.

"Wow, so you were duped as a child and as an adult," he said.

That she didn't take too kindly. Already things were tense between them and that remark didn't make things any better.

"Do you watch those ghost hunter shows on television?"

Oh my God, things were getting way too close to the truth here. How could she steer the conversation in another direction, but he was gazing at her intently and she had to answer.

"Yes," she said.

Travis scowled. "I'd never watch that stuff. It's fake. It's fake reality television. They tried to get us to agree to film here and the board voted no. Thank goodness. I could not have put up with their film crews filming the ranch. Telling nonsense about our cabins."

When was he going to realize she was part of that show? That she was part of the crew that wanted to shoot here?

She didn't respond but waited a minute hoping to change their conversation.

"What time does the rodeo start this evening?"

"About six," he said. "Are you going to participate? I bet you're a fine barrel racer."

"No," she said, knowing that just as soon as she could slip away, she was going to go visit the old homestead and then the cemetery where her father was buried. The week would soon be over and she needed to at least go by and visit where she'd spent her childhood. Put flowers on her father's grave.

"What about you?" she asked, thankful they were no longer talking about ghosts.

"I'll be there. I help out with the calf roping and some other events, but most of it is run by the ranch hands," he said, gazing at her, staring at her breasts. "Nice suit."

The way his eyes roamed over her top let her know he was still interested in her. And as much as she was attracted to him, it would not be good to pursue those feelings.

"Even for a carrot top?"

He reached over and grabbed her hand. There were other guests around the pool and she knew he couldn't do anything else. Yet, the feel of his hand on hers sent that tingling straight to her center.

"The carrot top has become a beautiful swan. Oh, and by the way, there will be a reporter here this evening who would like to take pictures. I thought it would be good for the rest of the school to see how the girl they made fun of is now prom queen."

Fear gripped her and she knew she couldn't say much, because if she protested, he'd wonder why. But she didn't need someone to see her picture and recognize her as the girl who did the ghost hunting show on television.

Shit!

She didn't need to see the bitches who had terrorized her as a child. Frankly, she didn't care what they did. They were in her past and that's where she wanted to keep them.

"I would have preferred to slip out of town without being noticed, but hopefully by the time he prints the paper, I'll be gone. And then all those phony bitches won't try to be nice to me."

He laughed. "Well, some may show up here tonight. Sometimes the locals come out to see our small little rodeo. Something to do on a Thursday night."

"Great," she said, trying to keep the grimace off her face. Why in the world would he do this?

"Gotta go," he said rising. "We're setting up the arena for tonight. See you then. Why don't you wear that bathing suit tonight? I'll give you a sash that says *beauty queen*."

"Why don't you kiss my ass," she said, glancing down at her book.

He chuckled. "If we didn't have a crowd, I'd do more than kiss your ass."

Warmth flooded her and she shook her head and closed her eyes. The very thought of him kissing her ass had the mariachi band playing in her head.

"Go to work, cowboy," she said and picked up her book.

Things were better between them, but not like they were before. Now that he knew who she was, she felt like she was walking a tightrope, and that soon, he'd learn about her show.

It was only a matter of time, and yet if she told him, he would have her out of here within the hour.

Could they get back to that sweet spot before she had to leave on Saturday? Did she want to get back to that place where all she wanted was for him to lay her down and have his way with her?

"Yes, ma'am," he said, grinning at her which she did her best to ignore. "See you tonight."

She heard his boots crunching against the grass as he walked away. How soon could she skip out of this rodeo? Maybe before the photographer started taking pictures? She didn't give two hoots about the girls from her elementary school who had enjoyed tormenting her.

Even if they were all grown up.

Or getting her picture in the paper. None of that mattered.

As much as she tried not to hold grudges against the bitches, she still felt angry for that little girl who had endured so much of their viperous tongues.

CHAPTER 17

It was late afternoon and the rodeo was in full swing. It started with Mr. Stephens riding a horse around the arena with the American flag and the man had done a great job. For the first time, he'd even followed orders. Maybe there was hope for him yet.

When he stopped, everyone stood and sang the national anthem. Next up was Desiree's portion of the rodeo. She led the barrel racers out and one of their guests showed what she could do.

It wasn't bad, but they were not professionals either.

Next came the calf roping and then the part that Travis dreaded. The bull riding. Due to injury concerns, they would not allow the guests to ride the bulls, but they had some ranch hands and even a few locals who like to try their luck.

It was a dangerous profession that left many injured. Some permanently.

Samantha's father had died riding bulls, so he made his

way up the bleachers to where she was sitting, drinking a glass of wine and talking to a woman he recognized. One of the *mean girls*.

"MaryJane," he said, tipping his hat.

"Travis, you're looking mighty handsome," she drawled and flashed her blue eyes.

The woman was a lecherous snake that he did his best to avoid. And now he suddenly remembered her treating Samantha badly as a child.

The first week after Amanda's death, she dropped by to comfort him. It was sad that he had to remind her he was grieving and not interested in her womanly charms.

"Samantha has grown into quite the beauty," he said, sinking down beside her.

"Yes," MaryJane said. "Who would have thought that carrot top would become so pretty."

Samantha tensed but didn't respond. In fact, she ignored the woman and kept her attention on the rodeo.

"Well, I best be getting back to town," MaryJane said. "I thought that maybe Billy would be riding tonight, but I don't see him," she said.

The man was hiding in the back, hoping she would be gone before he came out. Looked like he just might get his wish. If she knew he was going to ride, she'd be waiting for him when he dismounted, offering to massage his aching joints after his ride. Really looking to be his next ride.

"Good to see you, Car—Samantha," MaryJane said.

The look in Samantha's eyes almost had him laughing. The woman looked like she was going to stand and double-deck her. And he couldn't blame her. It just confirmed to him how mean MaryJane and those girls had been.

Instead, she gave her a saucy smile that didn't reach her eyes.

"Toodles," Samantha said in a voice that was mocking.

MaryJane glanced back at her and gave a little laugh before she hurried away.

"Toodles is what the girls all said that were in the club together. Those of us on the outs were not allowed to use that word," she hissed.

Travis couldn't help himself. He laughed out loud. In her own way, Samantha had just gotten in a little dig at the uppity woman.

"Well, if it makes you feel any better, Billy is coming up in about two riders and he's hoping she'll be gone before his turn. The man considers her a viper. He wants nothing to do with her. Even my randy cousin Joshua who's known for chasing women avoids MaryJane."

Samantha's brows rose. "Joshua is a hound dog?"

He leaned close to her. "He's dated a lot of women and probably slept with half of them."

She shook her head. "And here I thought all the Burnett's were good men."

"We are," he said. "Some of us, though, have had to learn the hard way that we're not God's gift to women."

Some of his cousins had yet to learn that breaking a woman's heart was not good for their reputation.

"You can say that again," she said, not glancing at him, but watching the rider jerking on the back of the bull.

"Who's that?"

"That is my cousin Jacob," he said. "Good kid, if he doesn't get his brains rattled trying to be a rodeo star."

"I hate this sport," she said with vehemence.

How could he blame her since her father had died riding a bull? There were only about four more riders before the rodeo would end.

"Understand," he said. "Bull riding is extremely dangerous and we don't allow our guests to try it out."

She gazed at him and took a sip of wine. "Would you let me sit on a bull in the pens?"

"No," he said. "Even that's dangerous. One slip and you're dead."

With a sigh, she shook her head. "I've often wondered what my daddy loved about this sport."

The rider was thrown and the crowd groaned as the clowns ran out to distract the bull away from the fallen man. Even being a clown was dangerous. Many of them had suffered from the bull chasing them or their horns slashing their legs as they climbed the fence.

"Most men find it a challenge. You're riding an eight-hundred-pound animal who wants you off his back any way he can get rid of you."

He didn't say the word gore because he remembered that's what happened with her father. The bull turned on him while he was down and gored him. Even though they had clowns to distract the bull while the rider got up, sometimes the animal set his intent on the rider. And Jimmy Griffin hadn't stood a chance when the bull turned on him while he was lying helpless on the ground.

She set the empty wine glass down next to another on the bench and pulled out her car keys.

"Going somewhere?"

"Yeah, I want to spend this evening visiting my family's farmhouse and even go by the cemetery and say hello to my father."

A trickle of fear spiraled through him. There were two empty wine glasses and the food had not been served. The announcer said the name of the next rider and he felt torn between staying or keeping her from driving off somewhere alone.

"No," he said and grabbed her keys before she could stop him.

"What are you doing?" she said, raising her voice, her big sapphire eyes glaring at him. The woman pushed back her long auburn hair like she was preparing for a battle.

"I'll take you," he said and grabbed her hand, pulling her from the bleachers.

The people around them were watching and he smiled at them.

"Enjoying the show, Mr. Stephens?"

"Why, yes," the man said, startled.

"Good, the next rider is thinking of going professional. Watch him closely," he said as he pulled Samantha down the steps.

"Come on," he said, hoping she wouldn't make a scene, knowing he was leaving the burden of taking care of the animals and cleaning up to his cousins. But damn, he deserved some pleasure time.

When they had climbed down the rows and walked a

short distance away, he hit the clicker button so he would know which rental car belonged to her.

"I didn't invite you. And I don't need your help," she said, pulling, trying to get away from him.

"Understand," he told her. "But you've had two glasses of wine and no food. I'm not letting you drive."

No, she didn't understand why he felt the way he did, but maybe it was time she learned.

"Of all the nerve," she said. "I'm perfectly fine. I don't need a designated driver."

There was nothing he could say to her response, but she wasn't driving.

They had reached the car and he opened the door for her and she flounced in. Yes, she was angry, but he didn't care. All he cared about was saving those long slim legs, her luscious curves, and smiling face. All he cared about was not letting someone he cared about get hurt.

He'd suffered a tremendous loss because of alcohol, he couldn't go through it again.

Tonight she appeared even snarkier than before, but he didn't care. The woman had survived some tough times, and he liked how her razor-sharp tongue cut. Maybe it was living in New York that had changed her from the soft-spoken child to the fierce-witted woman.

"Why are you acting this way?" she asked.

He sank down on the seat and started the car and backed out of the drive. She sat there almost pouting as he drove to the cemetery. He didn't know where her father was buried, but it was at the same resting place as his wife and baby.

When he turned into the cemetery, he drove the car toward his wife's grave, and Samantha frowned.

"This isn't right."

"I know," he said, wanting her to understand.

He pulled up in front of the graves and put the car in park. He got out and walked around and opened her door.

"Why are we stopping? Who is this?"

Taking her hand, he wished he had fresh flowers to put on their graves. He stopped at the marker and she gasped as she read the names.

"My wife and unborn baby were killed by a man who didn't think he needed a designated driver. I'm not going to take a chance on you being killed or you killing someone and destroying their life."

"That's why you don't drink," she said softly.

"That's right. Alcohol took from me what I loved and I haven't been able to drink since that day."

Standing there, his chest ached. The pain of their loss would always be with him. His baby girl would have been almost two, toddling around, and it wasn't fair that she had never had a chance to live.

"I'm sorry. Amanda was always kind to me," she said. "She even tried to get the girls to leave me alone."

With a sigh, he looked out at the mesquite trees that lined the cemetery. "We were so in love. After high school, we married and then attended college and graduated in the same class. Then we returned here to raise our family. I went to work for the family and she did speech pathology. We had just learned we were expecting when she was killed coming home one afternoon after working with a child."

When the highway patrol showed up at the ranch, he'd known something terrible had happened. One accident and he'd lost everything. In a single moment, his life had been destroyed. Even today, the memory of that day brought tears to his eyes.

"Let's go find your father," he said. "Do you remember where he's buried?"

"Over there under that mesquite tree. Mom wanted him there."

Taking her hand, they walked over to the tombstone for Jimmy Griffin.

"I should have brought flowers," she said. "It doesn't look like anyone has been here since his funeral. There are no flowers, nothing."

She stepped closer to the grave. "Damn, Dad, I've missed you so very much. Mom is still a real pain in the ass, but she never remarried. Said she'd found love once and she couldn't do it again."

That's how Travis felt, but her mother was older. Gazing at Samantha, he wondered could he fall in love again? Was it possible?

The wind blew softly and she stood there like she was waiting for a response, but there was nothing. How many times had he felt the same way as he stood in front of Amanda's grave?

With a sigh, she turned and walked away. "Come on, let's go. I want to see the farmhouse."

That was not going to make her happy.

"Before we go, there's something you need to know. That property backs up to Burnett land. Several years ago, the family that lived there forever, passed away. When they did, we purchased the land."

Shaking her head, she gave a little laugh. "Don't you guys own half the county?"

"Almost," he said. "But, hey, we're not land grabbers. We just buy property near us when people move on."

With a sigh, she crawled back into the car. Travis pulled into the small town of Dennis and into the school parking lot.

"I hated this school," she said. "The teachers knew the kids bullied several of us, but they didn't care."

Travis glanced over at her. "Maybe there was nothing they could do."

"They were the adults," she said.

Crawling out of the car, she walked around the playground and glanced through the windows.

"Mrs. McGill was my favorite teacher. She told me to ignore the mean girls who had no manners. Oh, how I tried, and then one day, I had enough and I picked up a rock and threw it at Teresa Adams."

"Homecoming queen?"

She laughed. "We were nine at the time. It hit her smack in the face and cut her cheek. Mrs. McGill told her that's what you get for tormenting others. Now go to the nurse's office and get cleaned up. I didn't get in trouble and I probably should have."

A brisk wind blew as the sun began to sink.

"Would you like to go to Catfish Cafe," he asked her out of the blue. "I'm starving."

"You don't have to take me to dinner," she said, glancing at him.

"Are you turning me down? The first time I have asked someone out to dinner in twelve years and you going to turn me down?"

It was true, he had not asked a woman to go on a date in so long and this one had started out rocky, but it now felt like a date. And he wanted it to be that way. There was something about this woman that he couldn't deny.

Something about her attracted him.

She smiled. "No, I can't turn you down. Show me the old homestead and then take me to dinner."

He grinned. "Gladly. But I have to warn you the house is no longer there. It was damaged beyond repair and we made the decision to tear it down."

"Just like you damn Burnetts to tear down history."

"Sorry, the previous owners could not take care of the property and it was in a shambles. Plus, we had a tornado come through that pretty much finished it off."

With a sigh, she took his hand. "There were good memories there, but it's been so many years. It's all right. Just take me by the land. I loved living there."

"Sure," he said, and they both returned to the car.

In a few minutes, he turned onto a dirt lane that led to where the old house had once stood. She could see the outline of the house in the dirt, but it was no longer there.

A tear trickled down her face. "If Daddy hadn't been killed, we would have remained here. But once he was gone, Mother was done. She wanted to go back east to her family and we did. I did not want to leave, but I had no choice. I loved living here."

"I'm sorry," he said.

With a sigh, she wiped the tears from her eyes. "So many years ago. Now, I'm starving, take me to dinner and then take me to Lookout Point."

It was the place where the kids in high school went to make out. He hadn't been there in years. "That's a promise."

CHAPTER 18

The night had started off rocky, but after they had gone to the cemetery, everything seemed to suddenly make sense. Now she understood why he didn't date. Now she understood why he was so reluctant to get involved with anyone. Now she understood why he didn't drink.

He'd been devastated by the death of his wife and unborn child.

After dinner, they got in the car and drove up to Lookout Point where she could see the Brazos River flowing below. The moon sparkled on the river and the sound of the water gurgling over rocks was peaceful.

Sitting here in the car, she understood why the kids like to come here and park. It was a perfectly lovely spot and very romantic.

She turned and gazed at him in the moonlight. "This is my first time ever to come up here."

He grinned at her. "I promise I'll be gentle."

"Maybe gentle is not what I want," she said, whispering in the darkness. At this moment, she wanted more of what she'd experienced in his arms. She needed more.

"Hot damn, woman, we're in a rental car that has a console between us."

She giggled. "Keeps me safe."

He leaned over and pulled her as close as he could. "We could go sit out on the hood of the car."

"We could," she whispered. "But only if you'll take off your shirt and pants."

Smiling, he gazed into her eyes. "You want me to take off my shirt and pants?"

"Yes," she said, thinking they were out here alone and they were adults. Tonight she felt daring and reckless. They were away from the guests, the dude ranch, and even the ghost. She wasn't certain how far she wanted to go, but she wanted to experience Travis.

She needed to feel his big strong arms around her.

"What are you going to do?"

"I'll take off my jeans and shirt. As to where we go from there, it's up to you," she said smiling.

The man cursed. "Wouldn't you like our first time to be in a bed?"

"Not really," she said laughing. "And who says this is going to be our first time. I don't have a condom, do you?"

She couldn't believe she was being so bold and talking about having sex with Travis. But that's what she wanted, but it wasn't going to be possible if they didn't have protection.

Stepping out of the car, Travis glanced around. "Neither

one of us has a condom. And you want us to just fool around out here?"

It was exactly what she wanted. What better place to explore one another than out under the stars?

"Just like we were teenagers," she said, stepping out of the car. She removed one of her cowboy boots and threw it in the car. Then she removed her other boot before she shimmied out of her jeans.

"Dear God, you're serious," he said. He lifted his hat off his head and ran his hand through his hair.

The car was still between them and she reached up and unbuttoned her shirt and slid it down her arms.

"I'm in my underwear and bra," she said. "And you're still dressed."

Travis stood on the outside of the car, gazing at her in the moonlight. "I'm trying to decide if I'm crazy or not. And I think you've pretty much driven me nuts."

"My job is complete then," she said laughing.

He tossed his cowboy hat in the car and then his boots and jeans. Next came his shirt.

"Meet you in front of the car," she said, trying to get a peek at his hard-muscled abs.

"Then what are we going to do?"

She giggled. When he was in the front, she took off running around the back. Thank goodness she'd worn some pretty underwear and a lacey bra.

"You're not here," he said, raising his arms and watching her.

"No, I'm not. I'd go running into the woods, but I'm barefoot and I know there are snakes here."

He started toward her. "Come here, Samantha. You've made me wait long enough."

"But the anticipation is the best part," she said with a whisper. "Just think how it's going to be when you catch me."

With a rush, he moved to grab her and she dodged him running around the car.

He gave chase, and finally, she tired of the game. When he caught her, he pushed her up the hood of the car.

"Damn, woman, you're beautiful," he said as he moved between her legs. He pushed her long hair back, his lips covering hers in a commanding manner that had her sighing with pleasure.

Why with this man, did she feel so many emotions, so much desire? How did she know that if and when they did have sex, it would be the best of her life? That it would ruin her for anyone else. And yet she felt certain that's how it would be.

His tongue swept her mouth in a way that had her moaning and pulling him in tighter. She could feel his dick hard and wanting between her legs and she pushed against him, wanting him, needing him.

They were almost naked and yet she knew they could not have sex at this moment. They had no protection and she wasn't on any kind of birth control. Trapping Travis was not what she wanted.

An unwanted pregnancy was not what they needed.

His fingers slid down her leg and she felt him trace the edge of her panties before slipping inside.

And then he was touching her. His fingers slipped

between her folds and her body clinched onto him. It had been so long since she'd experienced pleasure. So long since a man's fingers had brought her pleasure.

"Travis," she cried, breaking the kiss. She could feel his cock pushing against her opening.

"We can't. I'm not on birth control," she cried.

And then there were flashing lights shining on them in the darkness.

"Oh shit," he said pulling back. "It's the sheriff."

He rolled her behind him, trying to shield her from the lights that would highlight her near-naked state.

His body was tense and she could tell he was nervous.

"Nothing like someone ruining the mood," she said sarcastically.

The sheriff got out of the car and started toward them, his hand on his gun.

"Travis? Is that you?"

"Matt?"

"What the hell are you doing?" the man said relaxing. "You're not supposed to be out here—"

Travis sighed. "Thank God, it's you. We went to dinner and then we decided to check out Lookout Point."

The man started laughing. "We check this spot two or three times a night looking for young kids doing what you're doing. But I never thought I'd find my cousin here."

"Look, I'm sorry, it's just..."

What could Travis say? It's just that they wanted to act like they were teenagers once again. Young and stupid and so filled with lust for one another.

"No need to explain. I'm happy for you, but I'd suggest a

better place would be a hotel room. Less likely you'll end up in jail."

The man peered around Travis. "Who's that with you?"

"Samantha Griffin," he said. "She went to school here. Her father was Jimmy Griffin, the professional bull rider."

She noticed that he didn't use her married name and that was all right. It let the sheriff know who she was, and in some ways, it protected her from reality crashing down on her.

"Oh yeah, she and her mother moved away when Jimmy was killed. I'd say hello, but I think it would be a little awkward," he said laughing. "I just can't believe that I caught my cousin Travis here. You're not who I was expecting to find."

Travis sighed. "Look, man, can we keep this between us. No one really knows about us."

Samantha had all she could take. "Yes, I'm going home on Saturday. No need to get everyone all worked up about us if I'm leaving."

Especially his brother Tucker, who she was shocked had not found out who she really was. What was she thinking? Even the sheriff could locate her real name and what she did for a living.

"Do you want me to arrest her, so we can keep her here," Matt asked.

"What?" Samantha said, shock causing her eyes to widen as she glanced around Travis at the lawman.

"Samantha, it's okay, he's teasing," Travis said with a laugh.

"This is the first woman I've seen you with since—

Anyway, I'll lock her up so she can't go home if you want me to," Matt said with a grin.

Travis laughed. "No thanks, Matt. Just don't tell anyone in the family where you found me and what we were doing."

The man laughed. "It's going to be so hard not to. My straight and narrow cousin standing out here in his underwear."

"Ouch," Samantha said, slapping at a mosquito.

This had gone from being fun, to now she was frightened of the lawman and she didn't want West Nile.

"All right, I'm going to let you both go, but next time, get a hotel room. My partners might not be so generous and let you go."

"Thanks, Matt. I'd really appreciate it if this stayed between us," Travis said.

The man laughed again. "Another five minutes and you guys would have been naked."

Maybe, but she hoped they would have the good sense not to let it go that far.

Samantha groaned. "What a mood killer. I'm ready for you to take me back to the ranch."

"Good night, Travis, Samantha," the man said, laughing as he walked back to his car. "I'll give you five minutes and then I'll be back around to make certain you've gone searching for that hotel room. Enjoy yourselves."

"We're leaving," Travis said.

Samantha slapped another mosquito as they watched the squad car back out of the entry and leave.

"Come on, we've got to get out of here," Travis said,

then he stopped and pulled her into his arms. "Damn, he had lousy timing."

She giggled. "Yes, but another five minutes and we might have been so absorbed in one another that we wouldn't have heard him when he drove up."

The feel of Travis's arms around her was soothing, and yet her hormones were still on fire for this man. If they didn't leave now, they would be in trouble.

"That's true," he said. "But, damn."

Leaning down, he kissed her quickly. "We gotta go."

"Yes," she said, thinking she needed a cold shower.

They both rushed to their side of the car and quickly donned their clothes.

As they pulled out of the parking lot, Samantha saw the squad car. "Here he is."

With a sigh, Travis grinned at her in the darkness. "Matt is not known for keeping secrets. Don't be surprised if my entire family knows about this incident by Saturday."

And then when they learned why she had really been here, they would all hate her.

"Well, I'm leaving on Saturday and you'll just have to deal with the fallout, not me."

The words almost sounded uncaring, and yet she didn't mean them that way. But she had to keep reminding herself that she was leaving. If she stayed, she would have to tell Travis about what she was doing.

And that would ruin whatever this was that she could feel building between them.

CHAPTER 19

What a day! Samantha closed the door after Travis had done everything he could to convince her that they could continue what they started in her room, but they couldn't.

First, there was all her equipment that he would see, but the worst thing was the thought of Eugenia watching them. A little shiver rippled down her spine. Oh no, there would be no sex in her room. Not tonight. Not ever in cabin five.

Glancing at her monitors, she noticed that Eugenia was not around and was glad. Today had been nerve-wracking at the rodeo, gut-wrenching at the cemetery, and then the lovely dinner that led them to do something so wild and crazy. She couldn't believe she'd initiated them into removing their clothes.

What was she thinking?

Thank God the sheriff had been his cousin and not someone else in the department or they would be trying to get out of jail right now for indecent exposure.

And when that news hit *Entertainment Tonight*, she would be dealing with Travis learning the truth about who she really was, why she was really here.

With a sigh, she went into the bathroom and took a warm shower and then prepared for bed. Only two more days and her time here would be over.

In less than a week, she felt herself falling for Travis. She had never fallen for someone so quickly. Not even her ex-husband. But there was an attraction to Travis that she'd never experienced. There was a feeling between them that this was right, that this was meant to be.

And yet, it absolutely couldn't be.

Like her mother always said, if it doesn't come easy don't do it. It felt easy and natural with Travis.

And yet one big lie and deception stood between them. A lie so big and damning that she doubted that Travis would ever forgive her.

Just as she was about to crawl into bed, the EMF meter started going off and the smell of lavender permeated the air.

Not tonight. After everything that had happened, she just wanted to sleep. After realizing that the wealthiest man was attracted to her, she just didn't think she could deal with his great-great-great-great-grandmother tonight.

"Eugenia," she said, lying on the bed, just wanting to close her eyes and drift off to sleep where her problems would go away, "I'm really tired."

"Did you have fun with Travis today?" the ghost asked, ignoring her request for sleep.

Of course, she was ignoring her request, because she

could sleep whenever she wanted. Samantha's time was much more limited.

"Yes," she said groggily, determined to drift off. "We went to dinner together."

The woman's eyes danced with delight and she clapped her hands together. Suddenly Samantha realized what the woman was doing.

She sat straight up in bed.

While she had just realized she was falling for Travis, that didn't mean she intended to act on those feelings. And Eugenia was encouraging, and had been all along manipulating her to become involved with the man.

"Oh no, you're not matchmaking us," Samantha said, staring at the woman, her body suddenly tense, the sleepiness she'd felt disappeared.

"But, dear, you're perfect for him. I've been watching the two of you and no one since Amanda's death has intrigued him like you do. You stand up to him. The man has more money than God and you're not a woman who is only interested in his gold. The two of you go together."

But there were so many lies between them that once he learned the truth, he would never trust her again. This was not a good idea. It was the kind of plan that would only leave Travis heartbroken.

Not to mention her own heartbreak.

"Eugenia, I came here for all the wrong reasons. When Travis finds out, he'll be so hurt," she said. "Please don't do this to us."

The last thing she'd intended to do was fall in love with one of the Burnetts. To fall in love with a man who would hate her once he realized who she was and what she meant to do with her footage.

The woman took a step back. "What reasons did you come here?"

"I came here to find you. You were so kind to me when I was a child and I needed to see that you were real. I needed to tell you thank you and also I wanted to capture proof of you. All this time, I've been recording you, so that I can put you on my ghost hunting show. You're the reason I'm who I am today."

The woman looked confused. "You were a child and I just wanted to comfort you that day."

"Thank you," Samantha said, wishing she'd stayed in New York and gone to that hotel in Colorado. "I was so stunned that you comforted me when I so badly needed it. After that, I made the decision to learn about ghosts. You're why I have the career I have today."

Eugenia frowned. "What are you talking about? A ghost hunting show. I'm just an old woman who can't let go of her family, who wants to make certain they all find love and are happy. To make certain the Burnett line continues. I know I'm dead, but I can't let go."

How did you explain to someone over one hundred years old about television and how you were the host of a reality show? She had no clue about modern technology. Samantha wasn't even sure that the woman knew she was a ghost. She knew she was dead, but did she realize what she was doing?

"My daughter-in-law Rose thought she wanted to be an actress, but after she appeared on stage, she didn't enjoy the traveling. Is that what you're talking about? Are you an actress?"

In some ways she was, but she was more an entertainment journalist with a television show, but Eugenia would not understand.

"Not exactly," Samantha said. She pointed to the camera. "This camera has been recording us every time you came to visit. When I return to New York, I will put it on television and everyone in America will see you."

Clapping her hands, Eugenia smiled. "Well, I've always wanted to be the center of attention. Is that what this is going to be like?"

"Yes," Samantha said, but she knew it would not be in a good way. The rest of the family would have to endure more ghost hunters looking to find Eugenia. That was the part that the entire Burnett family would not appreciate—making Eugenia a star.

The ghost laughed. "Good. But first, we need to get you and Travis together."

Only problem was that once Travis learned of her treachery, he would reject her. And so would the rest of the family.

"Travis and the board turned down my show to come here and find you. He's going to be so upset when he finds out what I'm doing."

Eugenia floated into a nearby chair and frowned. "This is not good. I know Travis does not like to be lied to. You can't have respect without trust, child, and you can't have love without trust. If you're lying to him, it's going to be so hard to get you two together. He's been hurt so badly, please don't hurt him again."

And that was the part she was grappling with. She didn't want to hurt Travis or the Burnett family, but her career came first.

If she didn't produce evidence, she knew the boss hole would fire her.

"I know. Travis is a wonderful man, but I suck at relationships."

"Suck? Explain that term to me? Like a baby sucking? You can't still be on the tit."

Laughter erupted from Samantha. The ghost didn't understand the use of the word.

"No, Eugenia, I've been off the tit for many, many years."

Oh my goodness, there was so much Eugenia didn't understand about the current day and yet she couldn't explain everything to her.

"It means I'm not good at being married. My first husband left me because I put my work first. When Travis learns what I'm doing with you, then he will end what we have and kick me off the ranch. Once again, I have put my job first instead of putting him first," she said softly, realizing that she'd made the same mistake. "But if I hadn't come here, I would never have met him again."

She was falling in love with this man, and realizing at the same time, she had once again destroyed her chances at a relationship. No wonder her ex-husband divorced her and had a woman on the side.

There would never be happiness for her until she gave up her career and that wasn't possible right now.

"Dear, this is easy. You need to give up your career. Give up filming and I'm sure Travis will forgive you."

But it wasn't that simple. In fact, sitting here talking to Eugenia, she knew what she had to do. And it wasn't going to be easy. It would be damn hard.

"Do you love him?"

"Eugenia, you have to stop trying to put us together. I'm leaving on Saturday and it will be over."

Once she got on that plane, she could put this all behind her.

"Answer my question. Do you love him?"

Her chest tightened with pain and she glanced around the room. Why had she thought this was going to be easy? Why did she think she could lie to someone and then put it all on camera?

And now she found herself in the biggest mess she'd ever experienced in her life. With tears in her eyes, she gazed at the woman she enjoyed speaking to. The ghost who had comforted her now more than once.

"Yes, Eugenia, I love Travis."

"Then you must follow your heart and be truthful with him. He'll forgive you," she said. "I'm so thrilled. There will be more grandbabies in the future."

Samantha shook her head. "No, he's never going to forgive me for what I've done. In the morning, I must tell him everything. And then I'll be leaving."

CHAPTER 20

Travis had seen the way his cousins were gazing at him today and smiling. He was certain the cell phones had been burning up with the knowledge of how Travis had been caught in a compromising position last night.

Nearly naked at Lookout Point.

So today, he was doing the one job he hated. Cleaning up around the pond. A guaranteed place to be alone. The one job everyone hated and no one would volunteer to help him.

There were stories about how the original Travis Burnett and his soon-to-be-wife had made love for the first time right here at this pond. But he didn't know if it was true or not.

Sometimes stories told down through the years were embellished and became complete lies. Back then, there would not have been a road going down by the pond and there would not have been a hay storage shed. Nowadays, he didn't know if he would make love here or not.

Especially with such easy access to the pond.

But then again, the thought of Samantha came to mind, and right now, he would happily copulate with her anywhere they could find some privacy. He'd even put a condom packet in his billfold.

The last time he carried one there was when he was in high school.

With a sigh, he took the net and scooped the pond. He took off his boots and socks and rolled up his jeans to his knees. This was why he didn't like doing this job and put it off for as long as possible. He'd given the task to one of the hands, but they didn't do it the way he wanted it done.

As he waded into the water, he scooped the pond, cleaning up the debris, the leaves, scum, and even some trash. Tomorrow was the big dance and all the guests would be dancing to country-western music and having their last taste of Texas barbecue before they headed home on Saturday.

Then they would clean the cabins and get ready for the next set of patrons. This was the way it would be the rest of the summer. And he would still close the dude ranch if he was given the opportunity.

With a sigh, he thought about last night and how beautiful Samantha had looked in the moonlight. Five minutes more and they would have been having sex on the hood of her rental car. Five minutes more and he would have been deep inside her.

They were too old for that nonsense. Yet he couldn't

remember having so much fun, and if given the chance, he would do it again.

In two days, she would be leaving. In two days, he would once again be alone. How could his body and even his heart become so attached to a woman so quickly?

With another sigh, he continued to clean the pond.

At the sound of a jeep coming down the road, he glanced up and saw Samantha walking toward him along the side of the road. The jeep coming up behind her was being driven by their youngest employee, and in disbelief, Travis saw him pull out his cell phone and start texting, taking his eyes off the road.

The jeep veered toward Samantha and his heart leaped into his throat.

"Look out," he screamed and started running as fast as his bare feet could go through the muddy, slippery incline to the road.

He reached Samantha just as the driver realized his mistake and the jeep spun out of control. Grabbing her, he pulled her out of the way of the vehicle. As the kid came to a stop, he missed both of them with inches to spare.

Travis's heart pounded as he glanced at her, his breathing harsh from the jaunt up the incline. The fear that had his knees knocking and his heart pounding.

"Are you all right?"

"Yes," she said her big sapphire eyes staring at him in shock.

Once again, he'd come close to losing someone he cared about. But this time, he could do something about it.

"Get out of the jeep," he yelled at the driver. "Get out

and walk back to the house. You're fired. You never text and drive. Never. And you're not going to kill one of our guests with your stupidity."

The kid climbed out and put his phone in his back pocket. "Sorry, ma'am, are you all right?" The kid's bottom lip trembled. "I know better."

Travis was so angry, he couldn't speak again or he would be yelling curse words at the kid. And he was just a kid they had hired for the summer. Probably only sixteen, but his days working for the Burnetts were over.

The boy handed the keys to Travis and then he started walking away. "I'm sorry, Mr. Burnett," he said, his shoulders hanging in dejection.

The summer hires were given rules and texting while driving was a firing offense.

"You're sure you're okay," Travis said, holding onto Samantha. Adrenaline flowing caused his body to shake from the close call they had just experienced.

"Yes," she said breathlessly. "A little shaken, but I'm fine."

"Well, I'm not," he said and his lips covered hers. His mouth said what his heart knew and his mind refused to accept. They had been reacquainted for less than a week and already he knew his feelings. The kiss was demanding, yet so satisfying as if their souls were hungry for one another.

Pushing her, he pressed his body against hers, needing her, wanting to protect her, and then he felt his bare feet slipping in the mud. Letting go of her lips, he flailed his arms and did everything he could to stop the sliding, but the mud was too slick.

In his bare feet, there was nothing he could do to stop them from falling.

It was a moment that seemed to last a lifetime but took mere seconds.

Samantha started sliding and she pushed against him, knocking him to the ground and falling with him as together they slid down the incline and landed with a terrific splash in the pond.

Dazed, he sat there thinking what else could go wrong?

Sitting in the muddy water, he glanced at her and she started laughing hysterically.

"Oh my God," she cried as she laughed. "That was the best ride I've had in years."

As angry as he'd been a moment ago, he couldn't stop the smile from spreading across his face. What else could they do but laugh at how they had fallen into the pond he was cleaning?

She picked up a handful of mud and smeared it across his wet chest. A grin spread across her face. "You look really hot, all wet and muddy."

Laughing, he picked up a handful and smeared it across her chest, his hands rubbing against her breasts. Her eyes darkened and he could see the passion building between them. It had been there for days. They had done their best to ignore it and keep it from taking over, but at this moment, that passion was out of control.

He laid her back against the bank, his body covering hers. "I feel like we're in that movie where the couple is rolling around in the ocean, but we're rolling around in Texas mud."

"I'd prefer it was the ocean," she said, her voice breathy as she wrapped her legs around him, pulling him in tight.

"Damn, Samantha," he said with a groan. "Maybe we should take the company jet down to the coast tonight," he said softly, gazing at her. "We could spend the weekend rolling around on the beach."

"I'd be satisfied with a bed," she said.

His chest squeezed tightly and he jumped up and pulled her up from the water. She was brown from head to waist and covered in the oozy, slimy mire from the pond. Her clothes were like a second skin and her curves were outlined and dripping wet.

His manhood squeezed his pants tight as he stared at her.

"Or hell, let's just do it right here," he said.

Just then a jeep rolled up with Desiree and Joshua jumping out. "You guys okay?"

"Go away," Travis yelled. "Get back in the jeep and leave."

He took Samantha by the hand, picked up his boots, and together in their wet, muddy clothes they ran to the jeep the kid had abandoned taking care not to fall back down.

"We're fine," Samantha called out, laughing.

"We're going to be the talk of the ranch," she said with a laugh.

"Do you care?" he asked.

"No," she said, gazing at him.

Helping her up into the vehicle, he looked at the shocked faces of his cousins.

"Go away. I'm not to be disturbed this afternoon," he said. "I'm not answering my phone. Unless there's a fire, do not bother me."

Their mouths dropped and then Desiree started to giggle.

She doubled up her fist and pumped it in the air. "You got it."

They got back in their jeep, turned it around, and drove off. He knew the next time he saw them, everyone would know what they did this afternoon, but he didn't care. Nothing mattered but this afternoon. Nothing mattered but the time he spent in Samantha's arms.

"Let's go," he said.

CHAPTER 21

A fire was burning inside of Samantha. A flame she knew only Travis could extinguish. Never had she wanted someone so badly. Never had she been so needy.

Only for Travis.

She could tell he was pushing the jeep as fast as he dared over the dirt roads. She had no idea where he was going, but when he pulled up in front of a modest brick home, she glanced at him.

"Yours?"

"Yes, I built it after Amanda died," he said.

He put the jeep in park and climbed out. Suddenly she grew nervous.

She glanced down at her wet muddy clothes. "I don't think you want me going into your home like this."

He took her by the hand and led her around the back of the house to a beautiful, shaded porch area that had an outdoor shower and a hot tub.

Turning on the spray, he pulled her beneath the water

with him. The water was warm. And he rinsed off her hair, arms, chest, and legs before he began to rinse off his own body.

While he used the spray on his body, she began to unbutton his shirt, anxious to see his hard muscled chest. To feel the silkiness of his flesh. The wetness of her fingers slipped on the buttons. Her nerves caused her hands to shake.

Glancing at her, his emerald eyes had turned a darker color, filled with passion for her. And she felt the same.

Lifting up onto her tiptoes, she kissed his mouth and then worked her way down his neck, his chest, until she slipped down on her knees and unbuttoned his jeans.

Never before had she been such a wanton, but she didn't care.

"Samantha," he said with a moan.

"Yes, Travis," she said, knowing there was nothing more that she wanted at this moment but him.

"You said a bed. Beds are comfortable," he said as he pulled her to her feet and began to unbutton her blouse. "Besides, ladies first."

She grinned and reached down and rubbed her fingers on the outside of his jeans. His penis was rock solid and she glanced up at him and grinned.

"You're being a tease," he said with a gasp.

"Only for you," she whispered.

He leaned toward her, and she met him halfway, his lips barely touching hers before he broke away. It was a gentle promise of more to come that left her aching with want.

Their eyes locked in a not-too-subtle exchange that left

no doubt what he was feeling. She was lost to the sensations his touch evoked as he reached inside her blouse and caressed her breast. She knew there was no turning back, there was no more denying that she hungered for Travis's touch.

She wanted to be in his arms. Right here with his hands touching her.

Since last night, she'd dreamed of being surrounded by his touch, his smell, the hard contours of his body.

Sliding his shirt off, his muscles rippled beneath her stroke, and she sighed as her fingers traced the length of his chest, feeling his tight abs.

Still locked in a staring battle, he gasped, "The mud ... let me finish rinsing the mud off you."

His hands slid the wet material of her shirt down over her shoulders, down her arms. She stood before him, in her bra, soaking wet, her nipples peeking through the clinging material.

But she didn't care. This was where she was meant to be.

He began sluicing water on her, trailing his hands down her arms, cleaning the mud off. She did the same for him, running her hands down his muscular arms, reveling in the feel of his skin, aching to let her lips trail where her fingertips had lingered.

Suddenly he stopped, his fingers moving down her arm, leaving behind a trail of goose bumps. "I think that's all."

She gazed up at him. His eyes were almost glassy as they shone with a fire that drew her to his flame. He was mere inches from her, and she suddenly was nervous about what came next.

She moaned a soft, delicate sound. His hands went around to the back of the skirt she wore and quickly he unhooked the waist, letting the garment sag to the ground.

She stood before him, her bra and panties clinging to her skin like a lover. The front dipped low to expose the swells of her full breasts, her nipples rock hard begging for his touch.

She reached out a tentative hand and ran it down the front of his chest, down to his pants, her eyes trailing her fingers. At the waistband, she hesitated, glancing at him shyly.

"If you don't touch me soon, I'm going to burst."

Her hands were shaking as she slowly unzipped his pants; his manhood strained against the snugness of his clothes, eager to get to her. She tugged on his pants, and they fell to the ground in a puddle around his feet. He stepped from them and kicked the garment out of the way.

With a quick yank, his underwear was gone and he stood before her, naked and needy. His penis hard and rigid.

Raising her hand to his lips, he kissed the center of her palm. His other hand wrapped around her waist, pulling her closer, pressing her against him, her feet between his legs.

His penis slid between her thighs.

With a sigh, she felt like she'd come home. That this was where she belonged.

His fingers found the clasp on her bra and he peeled the

wet garment from her shoulders, exposing the tops of her creamy breasts, and finally her aching nipples.

Travis sighed and put his lips to the puckered tip, tenderly sucking on the tiny bud. She gasped and arched her back, trying to give him easier access to her breasts. He held her against him, his need evident and they clung to one another like two wet magnets, unable to relinquish the feel of him pressed against her naked flesh.

Oh my, how she wanted this man. Wanted him in the deepest parts of her soul.

He continued lavishing attention on her breasts while his hand slid down past her hips, removing her panties as she eagerly stepped out of them.

His lips covered hers in a kiss that promised much more to come. A kiss that tantalized her senses with promises of today and dreams of tomorrow. A kiss she knew would change her forever.

This moment in time would be with her forever.

She opened her mouth, accepting his unspoken acknowledgment of passion, wrapped her arms around him, pressing her body into his, sending her own message of invitation.

Travis lifted Samantha into his arms and carried her into his home. She couldn't resist him any longer. She'd tried—Lord, had she tried—but now, here, she had to have him.

She wound her arms around his neck, her hands caressing the sensitive skin below his ears, his pulse pounding beneath her touch. Slowly she ran her tongue across the naked skin along his neck, and she thought his knees would buckle.

"You are quite the little temptress," he sighed, stepping into the house, then into his bedroom.

Carefully, he set her feet on the ground, letting her body slide against his until she was standing. She stretched up and put her lips against his exposed earlobe. Nibbling softly, her lips moved down his neck to the tempting curve of his shoulder.

Somehow this man filled her empty spaces; somehow only he could relax her guard and slip behind the barriers she'd erected.

Taking her by the hand, he led her to his bed and she knew this was what she wanted. Lying down they gazed at one another, knowing this was a new, exciting moment. Eager and yet fearful.

Side by side, they lay touching. Slowly, she reached out and put her hand on his shaft. She clasped her fingers around him tentatively as if she were afraid he would break. Gently she fondled him, watching his emerald eyes widen with wonder. Her hand caressed him until she knew he couldn't hold back much longer.

With her heart pounding in rhythm with her breathing, she knew that if he didn't stop her, it would all be over in a matter of seconds. And she wanted much more, so very much more.

"Samantha, honey, we've got all afternoon," he said softly.

His fingers trailed down her breasts, past her waist, until she felt him touching the soft folds of her womanhood. She jerked when he touched her. It had been so long. So very long and she feared she would come right that moment from his touch.

Suddenly she grasped his free hand, squeezing as his fingers found her center. He stroked until she was moaning and wet for him. Stroked until Samantha was wild with need beneath him. Stroked until she knew she had to have him inside her.

"Travis," she cried.

She pulled back, her eyes large and dilated as she whispered, "Please."

He covered her lips with his, raking the inside of her mouth with his tongue, teasing and dancing, retreating and returning. Never had she experienced lovemaking so heated, so tender, so demanding, and she loved it.

Reaching into a drawer beside the bed, he pulled out a condom, opened it, and quickly sheathed his penis.

Sighing, she was glad she didn't have to ask.

He moved his body over hers until his manhood lay between the vortex of her thighs and plunged inside her.

A feeling of pure joy flooded through her. Never had she experienced the gripping sensation of pleasure that filled her.

With a gasp, she welcomed him into her body and squeezed him, demanding complete surrender. She wanted Travis like she needed her next breath.

Slowly, he plundered her and she met his every thrust with a need of her own. She knew she had fallen in love with him, but she'd never dreamed that making love would be so wonderful.

Never had she dreamed that as she stared into his emerald eyes, she would feel like they were one.

Rolling her to her back, he drove himself into Samantha with an intensity she knew he'd held in reserve. His lips covered hers in a kiss that sizzled with the fervor of his pleasure, creating a fire inside her she'd never experienced.

She writhed beneath him, receiving his thrusts, feeling so good.

She wanted him to devour her. Absorb her into his skin until they became one. As much as she wanted to keep this going, she could feel her climax building and knew he was close. Samantha lifted her lips from his and gazed into his passion-filled eyes. "Travis."

A shudder ran through her, and she tightened her hold on him, her eyes closing, her head thrown back. "Oh, Travis!"

She felt his release rip through him as he shattered in her arms, clinging to Samantha, as together, they spun out of control soaring into the clouds. The intensity was so strong, she moaned as slowly fell back to earth.

Spent, he sagged on top of her before shifting and rolling them to their sides, facing one another. Closing his eyes, he lay back, dazed.

Never had she experienced such lovemaking. Never.

For several minutes, she lay there stunned. Depleted, her mind and body slowly readjusted. She'd just had the best sex of her life, and it had been with Travis. The man she was deceiving.

Slowly, she opened her eyes and stared at the man she loved reveling in the aftermath of their lovemaking.

What did she do now? How could she tell him that she loved him and yet she was going to deceive him?

Rolling her over, he pulled her against him. "We're going to do that again."

She giggled. "Really?"

"Yes, just give me a few moments. I plan on not letting you out of this bed all afternoon. Then when I think it's necessary, we'll go eat somewhere. Then I'm planning on bringing you back here and doing it again."

Shaking her head, she caressed the side of his face with her fingers, the desire already building within her once again.

"We need to talk," she said, knowing she had to tell him.

"Nothing serious. I don't want to think of the future or anything else. Not until later, much later."

With a sigh, she pulled his lips down to hers. She wanted to enjoy every moment she could in his arms because she feared what would happen when he learned the truth.

CHAPTER 22

Travis let Samantha take the jeep back to his cabin. They had spent the afternoon in bed having the best sex he'd ever experienced. Nothing had prepared him for the way they had tempted and teased one another. Begging the other to take them over the edge.

And he couldn't wait until they did it again. He wasn't going to let her out of his bed tonight. Not until in the morning.

Sooner or later, they would need to talk about if they could make this work long distance, but for now, all he wanted to do was absorb as much of Samantha as he could.

They were both hungry, and he didn't want to be around the others. Not yet. This was too precious and fragile and new and he wasn't ready to share what they'd found with anyone.

So he'd let her take the jeep back to her cabin to clean up. But they wouldn't be separated long.

As he jumped in the shower, he began to hum. It was

the first time in years that he'd been happy enough to sing. He wasn't ready to get married, but he was ready to spend as much time as possible with her, even if that meant they had to fly back and forth for a while.

She needed to understand he would never give up the Burnett Ranch. Never.

After his shower, he quickly finished dressing.

The smell of lavender hit him in the face and he sighed. Good grief, he hoped his relative could not see his bedroom all the time.

"Hello, Eugenia, what can I do for you? I'm kind of in a hurry," he said.

"Travis," she said, smiling at him as she shimmered into view. "I'm so happy for you."

"Thank you. But how did you know? I mean I hope you weren't here lurking this afternoon."

The woman giggled. "No," she said. "I listen and then if I think it's safe, I pop in. But I'm so happy for you. Amanda was a wonderful girl, but she's gone. Now you have Samantha."

"Yes," he said, thinking could he get so lucky a second time.

"Just remember that all relationships go through struggles. Yours and Samantha's will as well."

That was for certain since she lived in New York City and he lived in Texas. And no, he wasn't moving.

"Everyone has secrets. You have secrets. I have secrets. Just don't let those secrets come between you," Eugenia said.

"What kind of secrets? Especially a ghost."

"That's for you to learn. But when you do find out, be kind. You must learn to listen and understand," she said.

Just then his cell phone rang and he glanced down at the number. It was Tucker. He really needed to take this phone call.

Eugenia began to dissipate. "Be kind and forgiving," she said as she disappeared.

"Hey, Tucker," he said. "What's up?"

"You're not going to believe this," he said.

"What?"

"Samantha Griffin Rollins is the host of the ghost hunting show that wanted to do a piece on the ranch. Ghost Seekers."

A trickle of alarm spiraled through him and he sank down into his favorite chair. This could not be happening. Not now. He was happy.

"What do you mean?"

"I think she's there because we turned down her show. It's a little suspicious if you ask me for her to come to Texas after we told her no."

His heart clenched. No, she would never do this. She couldn't.

"But she said she was here to visit her father's grave and to put the past behind her," he said, knowing that if this was true, their relationship would be over.

If she lied, he could never trust her again. That they were over. And yet now his chest was clenching in pain at the thought of her deceiving him.

There was silence for a moment.

"Has she let anyone in her cabin? Ghost hunters set up a

lot of equipment. Isn't cabin five the one we realized that Eugenia likes to spend time in?"

It was true.

"Cabin five is where Samantha was originally found as a child when she disappeared," Travis said, his voice sounding hollow even to himself.

Why did it feel like it all made sense now? Except for the part about the two of them finding each other and falling in love. But had that even been real?

With a heavy sigh, he realized this probably meant nothing to her. She was on the hunt for a big ghost story and he was just a pawn in her plans. What they had shared meant nothing to her.

And after this afternoon, she meant everything to him. Why had he opened his heart and let her in?

"I'm hearing stories about the two of you. Are they true?"

The whole family probably knew about them now. Once again, he would have to be the subject of tragedy. Poor Travis just couldn't win at love.

"Probably," Travis said, knowing that once again he was going to suffer heartache. That this time though his lover hadn't died. This time she'd just wrung his heart out and broken it.

Taking a deep breath, he knew it was past time for him to pick up Samantha. But they wouldn't be going to dinner.

The time had come to confront her devious ways and send her packing.

"Gotta go, Tucker. Thanks for calling and letting me know," he said, though he wished he'd called last night before they had spent the afternoon in bed. His timing was really lousy.

"I'm sorry, brother. You've waited a long time."

"Yes, and I don't know if I can do this again," he said. "Talk to you tomorrow."

He hung up the phone and grabbed his hat and keys. Time to send Ghost Seekers host Samantha Rollins packing.

Walking out the door, he gazed up at the sky. "Damn, Amanda. I should have known better than to give my heart to another woman. You're the only woman for me."

Stepping off the deck, he jumped into his truck and headed to cabin five.

CHAPTER 23

Samantha didn't know what she was going to do, but tonight she had to tell Travis about her show and taping Eugenia. This could be the end of their relationship, but she hoped he would forgive her and somehow they could find a way to stay together.

But Travis was filled with pride, and he didn't like liars and he'd given her his trust which she had betrayed.

It had taken less than a week and the cool, collected cowboy had managed to wrangle his way into her heart. She had never come here thinking of falling in love, in fact just the opposite. And yet she loved Travis and didn't want to lose him.

And now she feared how he would react tonight when she told him she was the host of Ghost Seekers.

Just as she slipped on the new summer dress she'd brought, the smell of lavender filled the room and Eugenia materialized.

"Samantha, you have got to be honest with Travis," she said, wringing her hands. "I'm worried about how he's going to react when you tell him the news."

A tingle of worry scurried up Samantha's spine. She was fearful too. "I'm going to tell him tonight at dinner. I tried to tell him earlier, but he didn't want to hear it."

She didn't mention that they had been busy seeking pleasure in each other's arms. Even she had not wanted to talk about her show while they explored each other's bodies.

Eugenia shook her head. "You two are so perfect for one another. He needs you and you need him."

Putting her pearl earrings in her ears, she glanced at the shimmering older woman. If any of her staff could see her now, they would think she was crazy. So far, Eugenia had been right about so many things she'd told Samantha.

"It's all right," she said, reassuring the ghost, and yet, she was plenty scared. Grabbing her shoes, she saw the headlights from his truck pull up in front of the cabin. She couldn't let him in. Maybe after dinner, but not before.

"It will be fine. Good night, Eugenia," she said, hurrying to beat him before he tried to come inside. "We'll talk later. I'll let you know what happens."

Sliding on her sandals, she picked up her purse and opened the cabin door.

Travis was standing there and he pushed her back into the cabin. He was strong and she couldn't stop him.

"What are you doing?" she asked shocked.

"Tucker called me this evening," he said as he flipped on

the light switch by the door. "Seems he found out more information about you. Told me that you're the host of the Ghost Seekers, that show in New York. The very show we turned down to do a segment here."

Stunned, Samantha took a step back. She could see in the dim light that he was furious. "I was going to tell you tonight at dinner."

"Were you?" he said, gazing at her suspiciously. Her heart was beating in her throat and she hated the look in his eyes, like she was someone he now detested.

"He suspected that you might have your equipment set up in your room and it looks like he was right."

What could she say as she stood there? "I had planned to tell you tonight at dinner. I tried to tell you this afternoon. I tried to tell you yesterday, but I didn't want to end what was going on between us."

The look on his face was filled with rage, his emerald eyes flashing, his nostrils flaring like a bull, and his mouth thinned into a frown.

"You should have told me the very first day you arrived here. Are you filming our ghost and putting it on television without our permission? Is that why you are really here?"

What could she say? It was true and yet things had changed and she loved Travis. She had no excuse. She'd been caught red-handed.

"Yes, that's why I came here after you turned the show down. But...now, I don't know what to do."

Travis seemed to almost grow taller and bigger as his eyes flashed with fury. "I can tell you what to do. It's simple. Pack your bags and get the hell out of here tonight. And don't even think about putting any of the recordings you took on television or the internet. I'm turning this over to our lawyers tomorrow morning and I will take you to the highest court in the land if you reveal our ghost. You did not have our permission to film."

A sinking sensation filled her stomach and she wanted to cry but knew that would not help the situation.

"I'm sorry, I should have told you sooner," she said.

She reached out and tried to touch him and he jerked back.

"You were the first woman I have felt anything for since my wife died, and all you've done is betray me. I thought there might be a chance between us, but now I understand why you're divorced. You're right. Your career is first and it doesn't matter who you harm as long as you get those ratings. Your husband was right to leave you."

He'd just ripped her heart from her chest. Why did it feel like she was losing everything?

"Travis, please," she said. "I'm sorry. Can't we talk about this?"

"Get out! Get out now. I don't want you to be here in the morning," he said. "And not a single picture better show up on the internet or you'll never work in television again. I'll make certain of it."

Whirling around, he stomped out of the cabin.

Sinking down on the bed, she put her face in her hands and began to cry. Why did she always lose at love? Always.

Why did this time feel even worse than when she

divorced? Because she cared about Travis and his family. Because she cared about Eugenia, and Travis was right. Once again, she'd betrayed them all for her career.

When would she ever learn to put others before her own needs? When?

CHAPTER 24

When Travis pulled up to his home, Tanner was sitting on the front deck. Just what he didn't want—a sympathetic family member. The phone lines must be buzzing with the knowledge that once again, Travis was a loser at love.

"What do you want?"

His voice was blunt. All he wanted to do was to get in the house, pour himself a scotch, and sit in his favorite recliner and watch mindless television that didn't show ghosts.

"Tucker called me and wanted me to check on you. He's worried."

"I'm perfectly fucking fine," he said.

Travis crawled out of the truck and slammed the door. He walked up the sidewalk to the front deck. Tanner was sitting in the rocking chairs he had purchased with Amanda in mind.

"Do you want a drink?"

Tanner jerked back. "You don't drink alcohol."

"Not normally. I'm not driving anywhere, so I'm self-medicating tonight," he said.

Tanner followed him into the house. "So it's true?"

What did they all want? Film at eleven of Travis ripping the equipment out of the sockets and tossing it out into the street? He'd considered it but telling her to get out was enough.

He couldn't face her at breakfast tomorrow or dinner tomorrow night. They were finished.

"Hell, yes, it's true. When I got over there to take her to dinner tonight, I barged into the cabin. There was all her camera equipment set up."

As Tanner followed him into the house, he shook his head. "But we don't have ghosts. I don't believe in that shit."

Travis started laughing. "Just wait. Someday soon Eugenia will visit you and then you'll be eating your words."

The thought of her visiting this afternoon right before he went to pick up Samantha reminded him. She knew. She wanted him to go easy on her because she knew that Samantha was deceiving him.

Why would she take Samantha's side?

"Let's just say I've had no extraterrestrial beings visit me. And believe me, I saw a lot of people die when I was in Iraq."

Travis poured himself a hefty dose of scotch and then he fixed Tanner one. His first serious drink in almost three years. But tonight, he deserved alcohol.

Together they walked into his family room and sank down in the recliners set up in front of the television.

"You're certain she was filming something in her cabin?" Tanner asked.

"Oh, yeah. I wish I had grabbed the camera and removed the tape. But in the heat of the moment, I was so furious that she was doing this when we'd told her no. I was so angry that she had not been truthful with me. We'd spent the afternoon in my bed."

Tanner's eyes widened. "Wow. Lucky you."

"Lucky me, my ass. My heart was starting to get involved. I cared a lot for Samantha and this is how she repaid me. She was going to put her footage on her television show and reveal our ghost."

He could just imagine the types of guests they would get after that. Everyone would want cabin five, so they could speak to the ghost. All the ghost hunters in the world would want to come to the dude ranch. All the reporters would want a story on how many had seen Eugenia.

No, just no.

"Maybe the tape is filled with nothing."

"Maybe," he said, though he knew that Eugenia had been interested in the two of them. She had been playing matchmaker, her favorite pastime when it came to her family.

That just made Travis even madder. And he was not the only Burnett to have seen Eugenia's ghost.

Travis knew his brother had gone through a lot in Iraq, but he also knew other family members had spoken to Eugenia. Desiree just told her to go away and leave her alone, that she was never marrying. It seemed that once you married, she moved on to the next person. At least, that's what his aunt told him.

Well, it was time for her to move on from him. This just sealed the deal. He would never marry again.

At first, he'd been spooked by seeing a ghost, but now, he just dismissed her. Especially when she started coming around after Amanda died.

"I'm sorry, Travis. For a moment, I thought you were soon going to be married again. You know we all loved Amanda and miss her."

He leaned his head back and took a swig of the alcohol. God, he hated the taste, but tonight he just wanted the drink to numb the feelings that had him aching, had his chest tight, his soul bleeding for what could have been.

The creek of the floorboard had him sniffing. No lavender. The ghost was probably sitting back hiding, waiting for him to explode when he accused her of trying to matchmake them.

Tanner's phone rang. "It's Tucker."

He answered the cell phone. "Yes, he's here."

He handed over the cell phone and Travis put him on speaker. "You were right," Travis burst out.

"Hell," Tucker said. "I was afraid of that. What did you do?"

"Kicked her off the property and told her I would be contacting our lawyer in the morning."

Travis could hear a concert going on in the background. "You're at work?"

"Yes, last show before she takes a break for two weeks. These are hell. Did she have cameras set up in her room?"

For the next five minutes, Travis told Tucker how he'd barged into the cabin and sent her packing.

"Any sign of Eugenia?"

"Nothing," Travis said. "Not since this afternoon right before you called."

Tanner glanced over at him and frowned. "Geez."

"Tanner doesn't believe in the ghost," he said.

In the background, he could hear Tucker laughing. "His turn is coming."

"I think you're both nuts. And you're not suffering from PTSD."

Travis shrugged.

"How are you doing? I heard you and her were starting to get serious," Tucker said softly.

This was the worst thing. Now the entire family would be treating him like he was about to go off the deep end. They would look at him with pity in their eyes, and at this moment, all he could feel was rage.

For the first time in years, he let his guard down and thought he might have a second chance at love, but instead he'd been duped.

"I'm fine," he said, knowing the way the words sounded that he wasn't fine. Hell, he was drinking alcohol.

"Oh yeah, he's doing great," Tanner said. "He's having a scotch and water. What does that tell you?"

There was a groan on the phone. His brothers cared about him. They had supported him when Amanda died, though Tanner was still in Iraq then. His cousins would have his back. He would get through this and move on.

But there would never be another woman in his life. He was done.

"Good grief. I'm in my home. I'm not driving anywhere. Why can't a man have a drink to make him numb?"

"That's why," Tanner said. "You don't do numb."

It was true. After Amanda died, he couldn't stomach alcohol. Not socially or privately. Over the years, he'd have an occasional drink if he was not going anywhere. And even then it was one.

But tonight's one was strong enough to knock an elephant to the ground. And part of him wanted to finish the damn bottle.

He didn't care.

For the first time, he'd thought of marriage and kids and everything he was missing out on with Amanda's death. Now, once again, it was evident he was not meant to have that kind of life. He was meant to be alone.

"I'm happy that you were dating again," Tucker said. "I'm just sorry that Samantha is a ghost hunter."

"Frankly, I think we should have helped her find that ghost," Tanner said. "We could have played all kinds of pranks on her and made her look like a fool."

With a sigh, Travis knew that was true, but he wanted nothing to do with the woman. They were done. Finished and now he just needed to let his heart heal once again.

"No," he said. "She's history. But I am going to call our lawyer in the morning and be on the lookout for anyone who might try to sell photos or videos of our family. If she tries to use what she filmed, she's going to have a fight on her hands."

Tanner sighed and he could hear Tucker sighing as well.

"Understand, but damn, I was hoping you had found someone," Tanner said.

"Me too," Tucker replied. "We're not matchmakers, but we'd like to see you happy."

Travis's chest clenched with pain. He would have liked to have seen himself happy with Samantha too.

Just then the bottle of scotch lifted into the air and the alcohol poured itself into the sink.

"You don't believe in ghosts, Tanner, so what the hell just happened."

He glanced at his brother and his eyes were closed tightly. "I can't deal with this. I'm going home."

A snicker could be heard.

"All right, Eugenia, you made your point. You don't want us drinking liquor. You owe me a bottle of scotch."

"Good night, Travis," Tanner said as he hurried out the door.

He could hear Tucker laughing on the phone. "Maybe we should let Samantha put her on television. Then she would get a taste of how it felt to be a celebrity ghost."

"Like hell," Travis said. "I think we should call one of those spirit guides who send them back and help a ghost rest. She needs to rest permanently."

"Good night, brother," Tucker said and Travis ended the phone call.

There was a hissing noise from his kitchen and he realized she had turned the gas on. As he rushed into the kitchen, he turned the gas off and glanced around at the mess she'd made.

The ghost had a vindictive nature when she didn't get her way.

"Damn you, Eugenia. Leave me alone tonight."

She materialized. "No. You sent her home. She's in her cabin crying her eyes out and packing. I'm here to make you regret that decision."

"Maybe she should have thought about being honest with me and telling me who she really was. We are trying to protect you."

The ghost rose shimmering in the air above him. "I think it's just an excuse for you. This way, you don't ever have to give up loving Amanda. This way, you can say you tried, but women are deceitful. Love conquers evil. I warned you and you took the coward's way out."

With a flash, she disappeared.

All of his scotch was drained. His kitchen looked like a tornado had gone through it and he was left sitting here, his heart broken.

CHAPTER 25

Samantha cried her heart out, knowing this time was worse than any kind of heartache she'd ever experienced.

Her heart was broken, and it was all her own fault.

This time, she'd thought she found someone to love forever, but she had screwed it all up by not being honest. And this could cost her everything.

Her job. Her abundant lifestyle. Her career. But most of all, Travis. She didn't think he would ever forgive her.

As she lay on the bed sobbing, she felt a delicate touch on her back. Not really a hand, but just a presence.

"Samantha, honey, don't cry. Things will work out like they're supposed to," Eugenia told her.

Once again, the ghost was comforting her just like she had as a child. But this time, Samantha wished she would just leave her alone. It was her own fault this happened. She had not been honest. She had tried to capture Eugenia's presence on tape and had even used the EMF meter to learn where she was hiding.

All of this was her own doing, and now, she had to decide between her career or the man she'd fallen in love with. Sure, he had threatened legal action, but she wasn't afraid. Every show she'd been on had some kind of legal drama going on. By the time they got to court, her show could already be gone.

The episode would have aired and long been forgotten, but could she do that to Travis and the Burnett family? To Eugenia?

But, still, if she had not met Eugenia as a child, she would not be here now. Yet, this woman had given her so much comfort and even now was trying to make her feel better. Could she show her to the world and have dozens of ghost hunters searching for a chance to see her?

"I love him, Eugenia," she said hiccupping. "I love him so very much and now he hates me."

"He doesn't hate you, dear, he's just hurt," she said. "You should pack up and leave. Give it some time. I'll be working on him from this end. Absence can make the heart realize what it gave up."

Samantha sniffed and sat up. The ghost was sitting beside her. "Thank you. Thank you for being kind to the little girl who was hurting so badly that day. Thank you for being here for me now. But most of all, thank you for trying to matchmake me and Travis. That means a lot. I'm sorry I screwed things up."

"It's not over yet, dear. I think you both just need some time," she said.

The woman wrapped her arms around her and though Samantha could not feel her long-rotted flesh, she felt her presence.

"You, dear, are perfect for my grandson. Don't give up on him," she said.

Sighing, Samantha stood and blew her nose and then glanced at all the equipment that needed to be packed up.

"I don't know what to do," she said. "Even if I give up posting the clips of you and me talking, I doubt Travis will ever take me back."

"Don't worry about it. Just pack your things and let me do the rest," she said.

With a sigh, Samantha pulled out her suitcases and began to throw everything into her luggage.

It took her over an hour, and when everything was ready, she glanced about the room one last time. This week had changed her, and she hoped it was for the better.

"Eugenia, thank you," she said into the empty room. "I hope I see you again sometime."

A flicker of the lights let Samantha know she had heard her. With a sigh, she rolled her suitcases out the door and put them in the car. Then she made a conscious decision not to tell them she was checking out.

Grabbing the box of tissues, she closed the door of the cabin for the last time.

Tonight had not ended like she wanted. In fact, after their afternoon of making love, nothing had gone according to plan. But she had loved their time together. Right up until he barged into her cabin and told her to get out.

With a sigh, she drove the car out of the gates of the Burnett Ranch toward Dallas and the airport. The sooner she could get on a plane and get home, the better.

A week ago, she had arrived eager to find her ghost and prove that she existed, but now, her heart felt different. She'd found her ghost, but she didn't know if she was ready to share her with the rest of the world.

When she arrived home, she would have to decide what she was going to do. But if her boss hole put pressure on her, that would be the worst thing he could do.

CHAPTER 26

Two weeks had passed and the pain seemed more intense. It was like every day he missed her more. It was as if a piece of his heart had left, leaving him behind. God, how he missed her.

This reminded him of when Amanda died. He'd experienced those same feelings. Only this time he felt betrayed.

Amanda didn't have a choice when she left, but Samantha had made the decision before she arrived to record Eugenia.

He'd contacted his lawyer who didn't seem all that concerned. For one thing, the man didn't believe in ghosts, but Travis knew better. And so far, Eugenia had kept her distance after pouring out his best and only scotch he had in the house.

He knew it was her, but what could he do?

It seemed like she was messing with his mind, moving his things around. His shoes were never in the same place, she'd rearranged his kitchen and even gone through his refrigerator. It was strange, but he was beginning to miss talking to his favorite ghost.

And yet he knew once she appeared, she would give him hell.

His family seemed to tiptoe around him and even Desiree came up and gave him a hug.

"Sorry," she said. "I'd hoped she was the one."

"The one what?" he said, irritated, even though he appreciated the hug. "The one to prove to me that women can be evil?"

She shook her head and walked away.

But the worst thing that happened was when MaryJane came to the rodeo and did her best to cozy up to him.

"Darling, I hear your heart is broken. I'd love to fix it," she purred.

"What about Billy?"

"Oh, honey, he's not interested in me. Besides, you're more of the kind of man I enjoy. I hear you have a hot tub. We could go skinny dipping in it."

The very thought of getting naked with her was enough to make him go on a permanent woman diet. And his disgust and hurt made his words curt.

"It will never happen MaryJane. Never. Toodles."

The word was not one he thought he would ever say, but it just came out of his mouth.

"Well, I never," she said as she flounced away.

Maybe she would never come back to their rodeo and he would be happy.

A week later, they had a new group of guests and there was not a single woman among them, though he knew he would never get involved with another guest romantically. In fact, he never intended to get involved with a woman again.

He was done.

Tomorrow, he planned on going out to the cemetery where he would pour his heart out to Amanda, though she never answered. Not once in all the years she'd been gone had he seen her or spoken to her, and yet his long-dead great-great-great-great-grandmother enjoyed tormenting him.

With a sigh, he warmed up some leftovers and sat in his favorite chair in front of the television. He tried to keep his mind occupied with senseless junk television so he didn't go to bed and think of the time he'd spent there with Samantha.

The memories refused to leave him, and he'd even thought of tossing out his bed but that was ridiculous. One night, he slept in the guest room, just to get away from thinking of her.

Just as he went to turn the television on, the smell of lavender filled the air.

Eugenia.

"Travis, it's been two weeks. When are you going to make up with Samantha?" she asked.

That was easy. "Never."

"What?" she said, upset with his reply. "No, no, no, no. The two of you are perfect for one another."

She shimmered in front of him.

"Oh, so you think someone who lies and keeps secrets is perfect for me?"

"No," she said. "I think someone who recognized she's made a mistake and tried to apologize is perfect for you. We're all human. We make mistakes. Even you."

For the first time in years, he'd opened up his heart to a woman and she'd trampled it. What kind of mistake had he made?

"Not happening," he said. "Besides, she's back in New York and I'm here. And no, I'm not going to New York."

The ghost was silent for a moment. "I don't think she lied to you. She just didn't tell you everything. She kept secrets from you and you don't like to be kept in the dark."

"No, I don't. Especially when we had already turned down her production company. You do realize they were going to show you on their television show. That we would have had ghost hunters from around the world seeking you out?"

The ghost seemed to almost explode in color before him.

"Did it ever occur to you that you were here to help her learn that her career is not the most important part of life? That family, love, and friends are more important than that crazy box your generation likes to watch."

She had said that her career ruined her first marriage. He'd flung that mistake in her face when he confronted her.

"Did it ever occur to you that she was sent here to help you learn that you can love again?"

With a sigh, he gazed at the shimmering image of his grandmother, the one who was known for matchmaking in her time.

"Did it ever occur to you that I don't want to be with anyone else? That the woman I loved died and I'm done with love. You can matchmake me all you want, but it's never going to work. I will go to my grave loving Amanda."

"And Samantha," she said. "Someone wants to talk with you."

His heart twisted with pain as she slowly disappeared.

The smell of a perfume he had not smelled in nearly three years filled the room. And he gasped as Amanda shimmered in front of him.

"Travis," she said, her voice having that funny sound she made before she cried.

Dropping his plate, he stood and reached for her, but his arms were only filled with air.

"Amanda," he said choking up. "God, how I miss you."

"Me too, love," she said. "I don't have much time. But I wanted to tell you to be happy. I was so thrilled to see that you had found someone else to love, but then you ended it. She needs you, Travis. Don't let her career come between you. Get married again, have children, be happy."

Tears streamed down his face. "But I love you."

"And you always will, just like I will always love you. But you also love Samantha. Go and be happy with her. You have enough love for both of us. I'm gone. Don't let my death make you a bitter, lonely, unhappy man. I would hate that. Go and be with Samantha. You need her."

"Stay with me," he cried, his heart breaking at the sight of the woman he'd lost.

"I can't," she said. "I'm not supposed to be here, but I felt you needed to hear the truth. Life is too short to be unhappy. Go to Samantha. Choose love and happiness."

She blew him a kiss, and in horror, he watched as she disappeared.

"Don't leave me," he cried, but she was gone, again.

Sinking to the floor, he didn't know if seeing her again had helped him. Now his heart was completely ripped apart.

Yes, he definitely loved Samantha, but he felt betrayed. She should have told him, and yet she admitted her career was her everything.

Would she be all right knowing that he still loved his first wife? That he would love her until his dying day? Yet, he also loved Samantha and she was here on earth. She made him laugh, she gave him hope and eased his sorrow.

They did need each other.

With a sigh, he stood and picked up the food from the floor and his empty plate. He dumped the food in the garbage, no longer hungry.

Glancing around his house, he wasn't certain that Samantha would accept that he would never move to New York. That if they were to make a life together, she would have to come here.

Could she give up her career for him?

Did she have to? He could accept her career as long as she was here and not three thousand miles away. Or he could even accept if they split their time between the two cities as long as he had Samantha.

As long as she did not show the family ghost on television.

What if she didn't even want him?

With a sigh, he thought about talking to his brothers but then decided this was his decision. His decision alone and it could blow up in his face.

Picking up his cell phone he dialed the number.

"Dan, is the company plane available?"

"Yes, sir," he said. "Where are we going?"

"New York, tonight," he said.

"I'll have it ready in an hour. Meet me at the airport."

"See you soon," he said and hung up.

Next, he dialed Tanner's number.

"What's up?"

"The chef is coming in two days. I'm taking some time off. Don't know how long I'll be gone. Can you get her all settled in when she arrives?"

"Of course. I've got to drive to Dallas tomorrow and pick up some supplies, but I should be back in plenty of time. Might spend the night at a hotel."

Why was his brother telling him this? He didn't care if he spent the night in Dallas.

"That's fine," he said.

"My curiosity is killing me. Where are you going?"

"New York," he said. "We've got to talk."

His brother let out a loud whoop on the phone. "Hot damn. I'm so glad. Can I tell Tucker?"

Travis sighed and gave a little laugh. "This only means we're going to talk. Nothing else."

"The way the two of you were gazing at one another. Oh hell, no, this means a lot. Go get her, brother. But tell her to leave that ghost shit in New York."

One day, he hoped Eugenia visited his brother, so he could see how their matchmaking relative made herself a nuisance.

"I'll text Tucker and then the two of you can talk while I'm gone," he told him. "And make certain the hen house is checked for snakes before you take any guests in there. We don't need a repeat of what happened with Samantha."

A chuckle came over the line. "I'm thrilled for you, brother. You deserve to be happy and she's the first woman since Amanda that's made you smile."

Travis knew the family phone lines would be on fire by the time he left for New York. Until he knew for certain that Samantha felt the same way as he did, he wasn't going to risk this being a certain thing.

For all he knew, he could be wasting his time.

"Nothing is for certain. We're just going to talk."

"What woman would turn you down? You're a freaking billionaire, you're a good man, and she'll be lucky to have you."

"A career woman might turn me down. She doesn't need my money and she's the host of a ghost hunting show. She doesn't need me. But I hope like hell she loves me."

CHAPTER 27

When you screw up big time in television, you pay the price. Samantha was the perfect example.

Packing her kitchen dishes into a box, she wrapped them in newspaper and wondered if she would ever recover from her time at the Burnett Ranch.

After she taped and labeled the box, she stacked it in the corner. Whenever she finished a box, she gave herself a small reward.

Taking a sip of wine, she picked up the dart and gazed at the picture of her boss hole that she had taped to her dartboard and threw the dart.

"Right there in the kisser," she exclaimed, claiming a little victory, feeling the pain of what these two weeks had done to her. Walking over to the window, she glanced outside at the lights of the harbor and the rushing of the yellow taxis below.

God, she would miss this view. This apartment. Her job.

But most of all she missed Travis.

With a sigh, she went back to the next cabinet, pulled out the dishes, and began to wrap them.

A lot of things had happened in the short two weeks she'd been home. A lot of decisions had to be made. And she didn't feel like making any of them. All she wanted to do was throw darts and drink wine. Only problem was the more wine she drank, the worst she became at darts.

And she liked hitting her boss hole's face. If she had a full-frontal picture, she knew exactly where those darts would land.

Fired. When she refused to give up the tapes, he had fired her on the spot. Security packed up her office and walked her out the door.

Not even her promises of going to the hotel in Colorado were enough for him to keep her. He wanted her footage. And she refused. It was now locked in her apartment, and the only time it would come out was when she wanted to watch again how Eugenia had done her best to bring her and Travis together.

Of how the woman had comforted her when she lost Travis.

It was all there on tape, and she'd spent the first two nights watching how she'd gone from being interested in the ghost to being involved with Travis. And somewhere along the way, she'd lost her heart.

Now all she had left was a broken heart, evidence of the supernatural, and her television career destroyed. With no career, she could not afford this fabulous apartment. And somewhere along the way, she'd lost all desire to be in television.

Right now, her only interest was drinking wine, playing darts, and moving in with her mother.

The boss hole had not even given her a severance package. Just fired her and moved on. Already she'd been replaced by the next up-and-coming television personality and they were on their way to the hotel in Colorado that had been investigated a thousand times.

He didn't want original, and she couldn't give him what she'd found in Texas. It felt wrong. Sure, she had lost everything, but there was no way she could turn over what she had of Eugenia.

The ghost that had comforted her. The family didn't deserve the attention their organization would receive. The ghost that played matchmaker would be a huge hit and all Samantha could do was lock away the tapes and never speak of it again.

Though she had been thinking of writing a book or a screenplay.

The Matchmaking Ghost by Samantha Griffin.

With a sigh, she plopped onto her couch and glanced out the window at the lights. She'd miss this place so very much, but maybe it was time for a change in her life.

Maybe she needed a career change. Certainly no one was going to hire her again. Boss hole had spread the news wide about how she had been dismissed.

But worse than losing her dream job was the fact that she had fallen in love with Travis. So many times, she'd been tempted to pick up the phone and call him and say, all right, the images are locked up. And yet every time she reached for the phone, she couldn't dial the number.

He would never forgive her, and she couldn't blame him. She should have been honest and told him the truth. She should never have tried to capture Eugenia without their permission, but in some ways, that trip had been for her. For the little girl who had been so hurt, and Eugenia had soothed that day so many years ago.

The trip to Texas had changed her. Made her into a better person, but in the process, she'd lost it all.

Over the years, she'd wondered if Eugenia was real. And now she knew. The woman was so real, and yet she wasn't a harmful ghost. No, she was there because she cared about her family. She deemed that they needed her.

The Burnett family would continue because of her insistence that they all find love and create babies. Lots of babies.

But without Samantha.

Placing her head in her hands, she let the tears flow down her cheeks. Once again, she had let her career ruin a relationship. Once again, she'd hurt someone she loved by putting her job first.

Would she ever learn that the person you love comes first? But she had never intended to fall in love with Travis. She had planned on making her career first in her life above all other things and then she'd met the man of her dreams.

Curling up in a ball, she didn't have the energy to finish packing up the apartment tonight. She lay there and cried herself to sleep. Knowing the pain she was feeling was no one's fault but her own.

She sucked at relationships. She sucked at marriage. She even sucked at being a career woman.

And now she was paying the ultimate price.

CHAPTER 28

It had been after three o'clock in the morning when the plane finally landed in New York. Taking a taxi to a hotel, he'd forgotten how busy the city was even in the middle of the night.

When he checked into the Marriott Hotel in downtown near Times Square, he quickly crawled into bed and tried to go to sleep.

But he was anxious about what would happen. Finally he drifted off to sleep, wondering if he'd just made the biggest mistake of his life.

Coming to New York.

The next day, he located Samantha's apartment, and while he didn't think she would be home, he went over to the building.

The doorman wouldn't let him in until he buzzed her.

"She's expecting you. Fifteenth floor," he said.

He wanted to say thanks for ruining the surprise but

kept his mouth shut and hurried to the elevator. Why wasn't she at work? Or did she work from home?

When he got off the elevator, she was standing in the doorway, waiting for him, gazing at him suspiciously.

At first, he wasn't certain she was going to let him in, but finally she opened the door and moved aside.

"Are you here to deliver a subpoena? Are you suing me?"

"No," he said, wondering if she had uploaded the videos. That would be a deal breaker for him. He had to protect Eugenia and the family.

"Come in. As you can see I wasn't expecting company," she said.

He walked into what would have been a beautiful apartment except that boxes were everywhere. Some were packed and labeled and others were open and he could see she was filling them.

"Are you moving?"

"Yes," she said.

"Where?"

"Connecticut," she said. "How did you find me?"

He walked to the window and glanced out at the harbor and he could see the yellow cabs all clogged on the street below. What a gorgeous view. So why was she moving?

"Your application for when you were a guest at the dude ranch had your address listed," he said, turning to face her. It was then that he saw the picture of the man taped to a dartboard and dart holes all over his face.

He walked over to the photo and started to laugh. "Who is this? Your ex?"

"No, that was my boss hole, Harry Miller," she said. She was standing by a coffee pot in the luxurious kitchen that had all the recent updates. A granite countertop lay between them.

"Would you like some coffee?" she asked and he could see she was nervous.

"Yes," he said, suddenly feeling more certain. Just seeing her was enough to make him realize how much he'd missed her. It had only been two weeks, but still, it seemed like she'd been gone forever.

"Why do you call him a boss hole?"

"Because he was always difficult," she said. "But he's no longer my concern. Someone else will now have to deal with him. And they have jetted to Colorado to search for ghosts at the same hotel that has been investigated over a hundred times."

"What happened?"

She finished putting the pod in her coffeemaker and turned to face him. "Do you like your coffee with cream and sugar?"

"Black," he said.

She went to the refrigerator and pulled out the cream for herself and brought it back to the cups she'd pulled out of the near-empty cabinet. All that was left was a couple of bowls, plates, and coffee cups.

He continued to wait for her to tell him what happened. After she fixed them each a cup of coffee, she led him back into the cluttered living room.

"Do you even know the reason why I came to the Burnett Ranch?"

"To prove Eugenia is real," he said.

"Partially. Remember how the kids liked to tease me and call me carrot top when I was a child? The school held our annual outing at the ranch one year. The mean girls were merciless in their bullying on the way there and even after we arrived. It was so bad and the teachers did nothing. They would glance at me with pity and smile like there's nothing they could do. Finally, I had taken all I could take and I ran away and hid."

"I remember them looking for you," he said.

She took a sip of coffee and her eyes looked glassy like she was tearing up. "I ran into cabin five and was hiding behind the bed when a woman appeared and comforted me. She told me the story of the ugly duckling, and that someday, I would be a beautiful swan. That everyone would be jealous of how I was so pretty. But more than anything, she gave me hope and made me feel better about myself. Since that day, I've wondered if she was real or if I dreamed of her."

"I didn't know that anyone besides family could see her," he said softly. "We've known about her for years. She takes turns matchmaking the single ones in the family."

Samantha wasn't throwing herself into his arms and begging him to take her back. They were both being cautious, and he couldn't blame her. But, damn, he wanted her to throw herself into his arms, kiss, and beg his forgiveness.

Maybe she was waiting to see if she could forgive him?

"Since that day, I've been interested in ghosts. I studied paranormal activity in college. I took journalism classes and studied to become the anchor of my own show. And all along, I continued to pursue ghosts. So for me, the perfect job was when I became the host of a new ghost hunting show. And I knew just the ghost I wanted to capture."

"Eugenia," he said, taking a sip of his coffee, wanting to reach out and hug her and hold her, but knowing now was not the time. Patience. He had to be patient or he could ruin everything.

He could lose her permanently.

"Yes," she said in a breathy whisper. "But then your family refused to let the show shoot on the property, and boss hole wanted me to go to Colorado and investigate in a hotel that has been shown on a dozen different ghost shows. It wasn't new. It wasn't exciting. And it wasn't Eugenia. I promised him I could get proof of this ghost and he finally agreed to let me go."

As much as he wanted to help her achieve her dreams, he was not willing to risk his family's ranch on her show. It couldn't happen. It just couldn't.

"What I didn't expect to happen was for me not only to connect with Eugenia, but for me to fall in love with you. I had no intention of ever letting another man into my life and my career was everything to me. But Eugenia played matchmaker and showed me that family is everything. Nothing is more important than the love of a good man. That you were beyond perfect for me."

"Samantha," he said, his heart wrenching with the knowledge that she loved him.

She threw her one empty hand up and gazed at him, her eyes filled with tears.

"I suck at relationships. I'm no good at marriage, and now I even suck at my career. Because I love you, I could not give them the tapes. So boss hole Harry fired me. Had security pack up my office and walk me out the door. Three episodes in and I've been replaced. I've lost everything. The show, my apartment, my career, and more importantly, you."

She began to cry. He set his coffee cup down and then took hers from her and placed it on the end table.

"No, you haven't lost everything. I'm here because I love you." Pulling her into his arms, he kissed the top of her head while she cried. "I can't live without you. Like you, I never planned on falling in love again, but Eugenia showed us that we're good for one another. She told me that you're here to show me I can love again. And I'm good for you, so that you can learn your career is not everything."

Slowly she raised her head off his shoulder and stared at him, her sapphire eyes shining bright with tears.

"Really? You love me? You're not here to threaten to sue me? Or tell me never come near the ranch again?"

Shaking his head, he pushed the hair out of her eyes and let his hand skim down her beautiful face. How could he convince her that he loved her?

"Samantha, even Amanda came to me and told me it was time for me to move on. That you were perfect for me and she knew I loved you. I do love you," he said, gazing at her. "More than you'll ever know. In one week, you snuck into my heart and made me a happy man."

She sniffed and then she threw her arms around him and pulled him close. "But I suck at relationships."

He tilted her head until she was staring into his eyes. "No, you don't. Maybe the man you were with previously wasn't the right man. Give us a chance, Samantha. If you love me like I love you, then we can make this work."

"Really? You want to try with me?"

"I love you, Samantha," he said softly.

"I love you," she said. "And if you continue to love Amanda, I understand. She was your first love."

His lips crushed hers as he pulled her body across his lap; his heart was filled with more love than he had ever remembered feeling. She melted into his embrace and he knew she would always be his. His little ghost hunter.

When their lips finally broke, she gazed up at him and smiled.

"Marry me, Samantha," he said with a groan. "Marry me and move to Texas. You can do whatever you want as a career as long as you're by my side."

"Travis," she said. "Yes, I'll marry you. Have your babies and be by your side until death parts us. And even then, if I can come back to you, you know I will."

Joy and relief filled him as he pulled her even tighter. "Thank God. I was so afraid you would not say yes. I've been miserable these last two weeks. I can't live without you."

"You're my love. I left Texas so brokenhearted it took me two days to get home to New York, because I missed my flight not once, but twice. All I could think about was how I had screwed things up once again. I won't do that again."

A chuckle came from him and he felt at peace. For the

first time in two weeks, he felt like his life had come full circle.

"By the way, I have the footage of Eugenia locked up in my safe."

A sense of satisfaction filled him. She had not gone through with her plan and had saved all the documentation where no one could find it.

"What are you going to do with it?"

"Don't know," she said. "If my husband agrees, I thought I could do either a documentary, or a movie, or even a novel, but not use the family name."

A smile spread across his face. "Thank you. As long as you never let anyone know that it's real or that Eugenia is part of the Burnett family, I don't care. I'm agreeable to whatever makes you happy as long as you're with me."

She reached up and wrapped her arms around him again. "All I want to do is make you happy. But right now, there is a big empty bed in my bedroom. I think we should test it out before I leave it here in New York."

Picking her up, he carried her toward a closed door. "You don't have to ask me twice. And afterward, I'd like to try my hand at darts. You know as much as you don't like your boss hole, if not for him, we would never have found one another again."

"True," she said. "And now he's someone else's problem."

CHAPTER 29

Eugenia watched as Tanner packed his suitcase. The man had a closet full of nice clothes and he was choosing T-shirts and jeans. The pants were all right, but the shirts were boring, ugly, and not at all something a woman wanted to see her grandson in. The only reason she knew that's what they were called was because of great-great-great-grandson James Tanner Burnett.

He had given her hell, but eventually, they all fell to her matchmaking abilities.

Shimmering before him, she picked up the T-shirts and put them back in his drawer.

He glanced around and she could see he refused to look at her.

"No, T-shirts, Tanner. Get a nice shirt. If you're going to impress a woman, you don't want to wear a thing like that," she told him.

For a moment, she watched him scanning the room.

"No, I don't believe in ghosts. The doctor said my PTSD was getting better. You're not real."

Walking to his dresser, he pulled out the T-shirts again and put them in the suitcase. As quickly as he turned, she grabbed them and this time, she refused to let go of them. He tried to pluck them out of thin air, but she laughed and moved away.

"Come and get them. But you don't believe in me, so just pick out a nice shirt in the closet."

Shaking his head, he ignored her and went to the closet and choose a nice shirt that she knew would make the color of his eyes pop.

"Much better," she told him.

"I do not believe in ghosts. Maybe it's the medication the doc gave me," he said out loud. "I'll have to talk to her about it when I go to the VA Hospital."

Burnett men were the most stubborn men alive. Until they fell in love, and they always had to be persuaded into marriage. But once they married, they were great fathers and husbands. And she couldn't wait to see who fate had in store for her grandson.

Tanner went into the bathroom and gathered his toiletries. When everything was in the suitcase, he glanced around the room.

"You're ignoring me," she said. "You can resist all you want, but there is a woman who will soon catch your fancy and I'm going to help you fall in love and marry her. I've been doing this for generations and now it's your turn."

"I'm damaged. All I want is a one-night stand. If you can arrange that, then I'll believe in you."

"No," she said. "I'm looking for a woman to be your forever love. To have more little Burnett babies with."

The man began to whistle the most irritating song, like he was trying to drown her out. Well, it wouldn't work.

"Travis is in love and will soon return. Now, it's your turn."

"Oh, hell, I'm going to leave tonight. I can get my errands run and get back here before the new chef arrives. And this PTSD will hopefully be gone when I return. Who knows, maybe good sex will cure it? Doubtful, but a man can hope."

"You can run, but you can't hide. You're next, Tanner. We're going to find you the perfect woman."

The man closed his suitcase and all but ran out the door. Eugenia watched him leave and laughed. She'd had many reactions before but never outright denial and her sighting to be blamed on something the war caused.

"Get ready, Tanner," she called. "It's your turn."

Once Tanner reached the car, he looked back at his small cabin and saw the lights twinkling inside. Oh, this was bad. This episode was worse than any he'd had in over a year.

He'd heard voices and seen lights flashing. Normally, he was sent back to a battle he fought. Always a really intense one where he thought he was going to die. But this time, it had been a sparkly old dress with a woman and the smell of lavender.

Just like Travis predicted.

Even his maternal grandmother had not worn that scent.

Getting inside his car, he locked the doors and called his brother Tucker. This couldn't be happening.

"What's up? Have you heard from Travis?"

"No," he said, his voice strained.

"What's going on, Tanner? Are you all right?"

"Yes, no," he said, feeling confused. "I'm driving to Dallas to pick up supplies and while I was packing my bag, I started hearing a woman's voice telling me no T-shirts."

Tucker started laughing. "Did you smell lavender?"

"Yes," he said. "Noooo…no…no. I don't believe in ghosts. It must be my PTSD. Something must have triggered me."

"Were there old matchmaking grandmothers in Iraq who tried to set you up?"

"Yes, but they didn't want the American soldiers near their granddaughters. Believe me, you don't mess grandmothers."

He stared at his house and the flashing lights inside.

"What else did she say?"

"Get ready, Tanner. It's your turn," he said, sitting in his car, watching the light show in his cabin through the windows.

The sound of laughter came from his phone. "I think you're the chosen great-great-great-great-grandson. Get ready, you're about to get matched. Are you ready for marriage?"

Shaking his head, he watched in horror. "No one wants

me. I'm a tortured man who lives in constant fear of reliving the war. No, just no. I don't believe in ghosts and I'm never getting married."

His phone was silent and he started the car.

"Sorry to have bothered you. I'm going to Dallas tonight, run my errands tomorrow, and then tomorrow night I'm going to find a woman and get laid. I deserve to get laid. And I'm going to do it."

"Good for you," Tucker said and Tanner disconnected his cell phone.

He backed the car out of his cabin's gravel drive. "I am going to get laid. I will never marry, but I can get laid. Hell, yes, it's my turn to get laid and that's it."

To Continue Reading Tanner's Story Go To Your Favorite Retailer

Jennifer Moss is having a really bad day.... But it's about to get even worse...

Her teenage son's grades have plummeted. Her husband is distant and cold, and now she's received a letter from the child she gave up for adoption twenty-five years ago.

But a knock on the door, spins her world out of control.

Losing everything, she packs up and returns to Mustang Island where the secrets from her past slowly unravel.

And the boy she left behind so many years ago helps her see that this new beginning could be the best thing that's ever happened to her.

But will their secret child unravel their relationship before it has a chance to begin agai

Contemporary Romance
Burnett Brides Contemporary Times
Travis
Tanner
Tucker

Return to Cupid, Texas
Cupid Stupid
Cupid Scores
Cupid's Dance
Cupid Help Me!
Cupid Cures
**Cupid's Heart
Cupid Santa
**Cupid Second Chance
Cupid Charmer
Cupid Crazy
Cupid's Bachelorette
Return to Cupid Box Set Books 1-3
Cupid Help Me Box Set Books 4-6
**The Unlucky Bride

Contemporary Romance
My Sister's Boyfriend
The Wanted Bride
The Reluctant Santa
The Relationship Coach
Secrets, Lies, & Online Dating

ALSO BY

Bride, Texas Multi-Author Series
**The Unlucky Bride

Lipstick and Lead 2.0
Nailing the Hit Man
Nailing the Billionaire
Nailing the Single Dad

Secrets of Mustang Island
Secrets of a Summer Place
Secrets From the Past
Secrets of a Runaway Bride

The Langley Legacy
Collin's Challenge

Short Sexy Reads
Racy Reunions Series
Paying For the Past
Her Christmas Lie
Cupid's Revenge

Western Historicals
A Hero's Heart
Second Chance Cowboy
Ethan

American Brides
**Katie: Bride of Virginia

ALSO BY

Angel Creek Christmas Brides
Charity
Ginger
Minnie
Cora

The Burnett Brides Series
The Rancher Takes A Bride
The Outlaw Takes A Bride
The Marshal Takes A Bride
The Christmas Bride
Boxed Set

Lipstick and Lead Series
Desperate
Deadly
Dangerous
Daring
**Determined
Deceived
Defiant
Devious
Lipstick and Lead Box Set Books 1-4
**Quinlan's Quest

Mail Order Bride Tales
**A Brother's Betrayal
**Pearl
**Ace's Bride

ALSO BY

Scandalous Suffragettes of the West
**Abigail
Bella
Mistletoe Scandal

Southern Historical Romance
A Scarlet Bride
Charity

The Cuvier Women
Wronged
Betrayed
Beguiled
Boxed Set

** Denotes a sweet book.

Want to learn about my new releases before anyone else? Sign up for my New Book Alert and receive a free book.

USA Today Best-selling author, Sylvia McDaniel obviously has too much time on her hands. With over eighty western historical and contemporary romance novels, she spends most days torturing her characters. Bad boys deserve punishment and even good girls get into trouble. Always looking for the next plot twist, she's known for her sweet, funny, family-oriented romances.

Married to her best friend for over twenty-five years, they recently moved to the state of Colorado where they like to hike, and enjoy the beauty of the forest behind their home with their spoiled dachshunds Zeus and Bailey. (Zeus has his own column in her newsletter.)

Their grown son, still lives in Texas. An avid football watcher, she loves the Broncos and the Cowboys, especially when they're winning.

www.SylviaMcDaniel.com
Sylvia@SylviaMcDaniel.com
The End!

Manufactured by Amazon.ca
Bolton, ON